CW00554229

THE PHANTOM WHITE HARE
AND OTHER TALES

THE PHANTOM
WHITE HARE
AND OTHER TALES

Alexandre Dumas

Translated by Douglas Munro

CANONGATE

First published in 1989
by Canongate Publishing Limited
17 Jeffrey Street, Edinburgh

© Douglas Munro
© illustrations Janet Pontin

British Library Cataloguing in Publication Data
Dumas, Alexandre, *1802–1870*
The phantom white hare and other stories.
1. Short stories in French, 1815–1848 – English texts
I. Title   II. Lièvre de mon grand-père. *English*
843′.7[F]

ISBN 0-86241-219-6
ISBN 0-86241-261-7 pbk

Typeset by Rowland Phototypesetting Limited
Bury St Edmunds, Suffolk
Printed and bound in Great Britain by
Billing and Sons Limited, Worcester

FOR ROBERT AND JO

CONTENTS

Translator's Note   *page*   1

The Adventures of Seven Stars on Earth   3

The Phantom White Hare   22

Peter and his Goose   64

The King of the Moles and his Daughter   81

The Magic Whistle   95

Original editions in French:
'Le lièvre de mon grand-père', 'L'Écho des feuilletons', Paris, chez les éditeurs. 1855.
'Le roi des taupes et sa fille', 1857; 'Pierre et son oie' and 'Le sifflet enchanté', 1859, all in Dumas' weekly journal 'Le Monte-Cristo'.
'Les étoiles commis voyageurs' in Dumas' daily journal 'Le Mousquetaire', 1854. All were published later in volume form.

TRANSLATOR'S NOTE

In his introduction to 'Le Lièvre de mon grand-père', to which I have given the title 'The Phantom White Hare', Dumas wrote that the story was told to him by his friend the Marquis de Cherville when, together with Victor Hugo, Dumas was in exile following the 1848 revolution in Brussels. Be that as it may, the original manuscript is entirely in Dumas' own hand. It should be remembered that Dumas liked both to mystify his readers and also to gratify those of whom he was fond and who had given him ideas for his stories. It may be added that de Cherville was the author of a number of works none of which, so far as I know, have been translated into English; in fact, I should imagine that he is now virtually unknown in France.

Again, in my translation of 'Les étoiles commis voyageurs' I have changed the original title to 'The Adventures of Seven Stars on Earth'. This is a reshaping by Dumas of a tale which originated from one told to him by a Viennese humorist whose acquaintance Dumas had also made in Brussels. This man was named Moritz Gottlieb Saphir who had been born in Hungary in 1795. An improbable name? But there was a reason. His grandfather was called Israel Israel, and when all Jews were ordered by the Emperor Joseph II to adopt family names he was asked by what name he wished to be known. He did not know and the magistrate who was interviewing him, noticing he was wearing a signet ring with a sapphire, suggested that he should call himself 'Saphir'. This he did.

Moritz Gottlieb was first sent to Prague to study the Talmud, and from there he went to Vienna. He began to write satirical criticism and pamphlets and two of the latter, in 1828, created a sensation. He travelled considerably throughout Europe and in Brussels, as I have said, formed a friendship with Dumas who, subsequently in the drawing-rooms of Prince Napoleon and Princess Mathilde told so many anecdotes about him that many people came to believe that Saphir was somebody that Dumas had created out of his own imagination. He died in 1858 in Baden. The satirical streak in his writing can be seen in 'The Adventures of Seven Stars on Earth'.

Except for 'The Magic Whistle' the two other short stories were possibly taken from German sources; 'The King of the Moles and his Daughter' was actually related to him by another friend, Gérard de Nerval, when they were travelling together along the Rhine many years earlier in 1838, accompanied by the rather mediocre actress Ida Ferrier whom Dumas subsequently married.

THE TRANSLATOR

THE ADVENTURES OF SEVEN STARS
ON EARTH

There was once a king who liked to think of himself as a poet.
But, as one cannot do two things at once, this king crowned as
he was with a golden diamond-studded circlet, was such a
dreadful poet that whenever there was a riot in his kingdom
(and that happened often enough and happened, indeed, once
too often when he was forced to give the crown to his son) and
the crowd had been called to order three times according to
custom, the mayor would step onto a platform which was rolled
behind him for exactly this purpose, and would read some of
the royal verse to the rather ill-tempered crowd. Should the
riot be a comparatively mild one he would need to read only a
couple of verses; if it was stormy then more verses were needed.
But it was rarely more than a third of a lengthy poem before the
mob, no matter how large, would melt away as if by magic.

Now, it so happened that I was travelling through the royal
poet's kingdom and was visiting many of the most interesting
places in the country. For although the monarch was not a man
of much imagination himself he was, curiously, quite a patron
of the arts. After I had looked at all the statues and wandered
through the various museums and palaces there was nothing
left for me to visit but the prisons. I was not particularly keen to
do this for I have no fondness for studying that type of art, if
such it may be called. But I had a guide given to me, one of those
guides whose hearts are made of stone, so I meekly followed him
into one of those gloomy buildings.

The prison in the capital of the king-poet's country was very

3

much like all such similar prisons, and would have been nothing out of the ordinary if it were not for the fact that it held no prisoners. In fact, it had had one not so long before who was to have been in residence there for some three weeks but had stayed for only three days. He was a journalist from Vienna, and finding himself in the king-poet's capital had made use of the chance to do something by poking fun at the royal poetry. The chief of police finding out who was the author took upon himself to arrest the rather naughty author and to secretly put him in jail. Not only this, but he ordered him to write a letter to the city's only newspaper publicly begging the king's pardon.

Luckily the king somehow learned what had happened. He immediately called for the state coach and to the great amazement of the coachman when he closed the door behind him ordered:

'To the prison!'

In about five minutes the prisoner was told that he had a visitor who was none other than his majesty the king. The prisoner had only just the time to slip into a table-drawer a story that he had just finished, and which also made fun of a king, when the royal personage came into his cell.

This time, however, the writer instead of attacking an earthly king poked fun at the ruler of Olympus, in the hope that Jupiter would be rather less touchy than his unexpected visitor.

But, after all, the king was not as thin-skinned as the writer imagined. He walked in, hat in hand, as any author should in the presence of his critic or, indeed, as an accused before his judge, beseeched the prisoner to forgive the rudeness of the police, and come and have dinner with him at the palace.

It naturally followed that it was impossible for the unfortunate man to get his story out of the drawer and take it away with him. So there it lay until its author had left the country, when it was found by the gaoler whose job it was to clean out the cell. In

4

due course the king was told of the discovery. The Viennese had by now returned to Austria.

The king commanded that the story be sent back to its author by a reliable messenger. 'And above all,' he said, 'be sure that it doesn't fall into the hands of the chief of police.'

But up to the day I visited the prison no reliable messenger had been found.

'Are you, by any chance, going to Vienna?' asked the gaoler who was showing me round and who told me all that I have told you.

'I should be there in about three days,' I replied.

'Will you promise to give these papers to the poet and writer who was locked in here?'

'Most certainly, and with the greatest of pleasure.'

'Then please give me a receipt for them.'

I gave him the receipt and at the same time handed him a crown-piece. That night I left for Vienna.

A couple of days later I called on the journalist and before we parted I gave him in exchange for his story one of mine. Six years had passed since my story was published in his paper; I had not forgotten his, but thought that I must have lost it. One day when I was turning over some old papers I came across some in a strange hand and at once knew that this could only be the story that had been entrusted to me by the gaoler at the king-poet's prison and given to me in exchange. Here, then, it is.

Very long ago when the heavens were called Olympus the god who ruled there and was named Zeus, or Jove, or Jupiter (these three words mean very much the same thing) one day had a strange idea.

This was to make the human race happy.

It will be seen how he was cured of this desire and how the other gods who came after him were cured of it too.

5

Nobody knows how on earth, or rather in the heavens, such a thought came into his head. But it is pretty certain that when Jupiter told of his plan to his favourite advisers, Neptune the god of all the seas, and Pluto the god of hell, those two worthies thought that the idea was so ridiculous that they cried out in one voice:

'Oh, your majesty, what a comical thought! By Jupiter, or Jove or Zeus, what an odd idea!'

But when a god gets an idea into his head, good or bad, he always sees it through to the end, even if it be the laughable one of trying to make mankind happy.

How was it to be done? Jupiter thought for a time and then, suddenly raising his head, exclaimed: 'I've got it!'

And he summoned the seven stars of the Little Bear to his presence. The stars hurried to obey. The people of the earth stared in amazement at the heavens, for, seeing seven stars shooting through space leaving sparkling tails behind them, they thought that the end of the world was near.

The seven stars cried out together:

'Here we all are, king most splendid and terrible! Why have you called for us?'

'Everyone of you will pack your things and set out on a visit to earth,' was the answer, and he went on, 'you will receive five francs a day for your travelling expenses.'

'But what are we to do on earth?'

'I have taken it into my head to make mankind happy,' Jupiter replied. 'But as they may not believe in their good luck if I give it to them for nothing I order you to sell it for what you can get. In other words you are going to be my commercial travellers.'

'We will obey your command, all-powerful majesty,' the stars said in unison, and in such melodious voices that the people on earth below again looked skywards for they knew that only such sweet sounds could come from heaven. 'But what will we sell to these people?'

Jupiter then commanded the stars to stand in line and pass before him one by one. The stars did as they were told.

Then Jupiter said to the first: 'You will sell Wit.' To the second: 'You will sell Virtue.' To the third: 'You will sell Health.' To the fourth: 'You will sell Long Life.' To the fifth: 'You will sell Honour.' To the sixth: 'You will sell Pleasure.' And to the last: 'You will sell Riches.'

Jupiter, judging by the prayers mankind offered up to him, thought that when men and women were allowed to have all seven of his commands they would be perfectly happy. And I think that you would have thought so too.

'Now, be off,' he said to the stars, 'and sell as much of your heavenly goods as you possibly can.'

But Neptune and Pluto were no more convinced than they had been before. They began to laugh more heartily than ever, saying once again: 'Oh, what an odd idea, your majesty! By Jupiter, what a comical thought!'

The seven stars packed up their seven kinds of goods in seven different boxes provided for them by the storekeeper of heaven, and flying down to earth started to do business in the first large town they came to.

'Wit! Wit! Who'll buy Wit?' called out star number one. 'Here it is, all fresh and hot. Wit! Wit! Buy my Wit!'

Laughter greeted the cry.

'Good heavens, does this silly girl take us all for fools?' said the journalists, the story-writers, the playwrights and the producers of pantomimes.

'She's a lovely girl with a pretty figure,' said the fops staring at the Wit-seller through their eye-glasses, their spectacles, or binoculars, switching as they did so at their boots with canes they held in their yellow-gloved hands. 'What a shame it is that she looks rather like a blue-stocking.'

'What is this little minx doing here?' asked the women. 'She would have done much better if she had brought some silks from Lyon, lace from Valenciennes, shawls from Algiers, coral from Naples, pearls from Ceylon, rubies from Visapore, or diamonds from Golconda. But, Wit! We can have that for nothing. It can be found everywhere. She will have to eat her own goods to keep herself alive, and even then she will die of hunger.'

And so the poor little star wandered along one street after another without selling any of her wares, until at last she came to an open door and went in without knowing where she was going. In fact, she had entered the Academy of Authors at the very moment when they were welcoming a new member. He had just finished making his speech of thanks and the secretary of that august assembly had risen to his feet to reply.

'Wit! Wit! Wit for sale!' cried the innocent little star.

Everyone burst into laughter but the secretary who, much put out, sniffed a pinch of snuff that went the wrong way and which made him sneeze for a good half an hour.

The president called to the attendants, and said: 'Put that stupid creature out and tell the door-keeper that she must never be allowed to enter the Academy again.'

The attendants pushed the star out into the street, and the door-keeper heard the president's instructions and obeyed them from then on.

Poor little first star went away feeling very sorry for herself. But as she was a well-meaning little star she wanted to do her duty as she had been told to do. After having walked for a short way along the quay she crossed a bridge and saw that she had reached an island. On the island was a public square on which stood a statue, and on the further side was a large building. Up and down the steps leading into it she saw a crowd of hurrying people, people who looked so very busy and so lacking in Mother Wit that she thought that this was the very place where her wares would be welcome. She could not know that the more stupid people are the less likely they would be to think that they needed wit.

8

The star pushed her way through the crowd and entered a great hall where three men were sitting at a table in black robes and wearing square black caps. On either side of them were other men, dressed like themselves in gowns and black caps. Then the star realised that she was in a court of justice, and that the men in black were the judges and lawyers.

A very important case was being heard and the court was crowded. The lawyer for the plaintiff, an ugly unwashed little man with a cheerless face and a flattened nose, had just finished speaking so that there was a pause for the moment as the star entered. She thought that this was a happy chance and called out cheerfully:

'Wit, gentlemen! Who'll buy Wit? Wit for sale cheap!'

Unluckily, however, both the lawyer who had just spoken and the one who was about to speak thought that this was some hidden joke which was being poked at them; they, for once, agreed with one another and blamed the unlucky star. The result was that the little seller of Wit was put into the dock and accused of contempt of court.

Happily, the senior judge was quite a young man with a good deal of wit himself, and so he was quite content to order that the star should be taken out of the courtroom by two policemen. The policemen took hold of the star on either side by a ray and led her out onto the street saying as they did so:

'You've got off with a fright this time, my dear, but don't you come here again.'

Poor first star went away feeling much puzzled. But as she had made up her mind not to leave the city without making a sale of some sort she walked, and walked, and walked until she came to another big square with another monument in its centre.

'Ah,' she said to herself, 'this looks like a temple that I've seen in Athens, and the Athenians have so much wit that I am sure that these people will be only too glad to buy more of it, too, at any price I ask.'

So she began to call out: 'Buy my Wit, Athenians, buy my Wit.'

Two men passed her, one holding a case crammed with pieces of paper of all kinds, the other with a notebook in which he was scribbling figures as he walked along.

'I think she called us Athenians,' said the man with the case.

'Yes, I imagine I heard her say something of the sort,' answered the man with the notebook.

'What on earth does she mean by "Athenians"?', asked the man with the case.

'It's probably some sort of a new society that they've just started,' the man with the notebook replied.

'Wit! Who'll buy my Wit?' cried the little star following the two men.

'Ah,' said the man with the case, 'another company gone bankrupt I suppose.'

And they both entered the Grecian temple which was none other than the stock exchange. The star followed them and marched through the noisy crowd, shouting as loudly as she could: 'Wit! Wit! Who'll buy Wit?'

A stockbroker came up to her and asked: 'What on earth are you selling?'

'Wit.'

'Wit? Oh!'

'Do you know what it is?'

'I've heard it spoken of.'

'You should buy some even if it is only a little, and if only to get to know what it's like.'

'Is it quoted on the share list?'

'No.'

'Then what are you doing with it here?' And he turned his back on the star, saying to a friend as he did so, 'She's not licensed to sell her goods, come away.'

They both went away in search of three other brokers, who pointed out the star to a police officer. He asked to see her

permit to enter the building, and being told that she had none
called to two of his men who took poor first star to the police
station.

The sergeant would have sent her to prison, but seeing that
the girl did not seem to know that she had done any wrong and
was a stranger (which was easy to see from the sort of goods she
was trying to sell) he did no more than order her to leave the
city within twenty-four hours.

The star was so utterly tired of all the rudeness shown to her
by the people of the first town she had tried that she saved
twenty-three and a half hours of that time by leaving straight
away.

But at the gates stood a tax-collector, and he stopped her.

'What have you in that box?' he asked sharply.

'Wit.'

'What did you say – victuals?'

'No, only wit.'

'Hah! Smuggling!' the man shouted, for he always said that
of any goods of which he had never heard before.

He told his men to seize the star, and she was fined three
francs and fifty centimes. Then two of the Customs men took
her box from her, smashed the little bottles in it, and poured
the contents into the gutter. After that two others grabbed her
by her rays and marched her through the gates, telling her
never dare to return on pain of three months in jail.

Ever since then wit has flowed freely in the gutter, and that is
why street-urchins who drink of it have so much wit.

Now, while first star was leaving the city by one gate, second
star was entering by another, calling out as she did so: 'Virtue!
Virtue! Who'll buy Virtue?'

The first people to hear her could not believe their ears. But
the star, full of faith in her goods, shouted so loudly and clearly
that some of the most unbelieving could not mistake her
meaning any longer. Some of them turned up their noses at her,
saying to each other:

'It must be some poor mad creature who has escaped from Bedlam.'

The rich ones added: 'They build such small houses these days that ours are already crowded with furniture, so where on earth could we put Virtue?'

The poor muttered: 'What could we poor creatures do with such precious stuff? It's not worth our while trying to save up and buy it, for if we did so no one would believe that we had it.'

The young said: 'Virtue! Why, we already have horses and packs of hounds. If we bought virtue as well it would serve us right if our parents turned us out of the house for our wastefulness.'

Only one woman went up to the seller of Virtue. She was the widow of a deputy sub-postmaster.

'How much does Virtue cost?' she demanded.

'Nothing.'

'What, nothing?'

'Only the bother of keeping it.'

'It's too dear,' said the widow of the deputy sub-postmaster, and turned her back on the star.

So the star, seeing that the people of this city did not come to her, decided to go to them. So she entered the first door.

'What do you want?' a sharp voice called out. A tall, thin, withered woman was sitting there and her dog, which looked as ill-natured as its owner, began barking at the stranger.

'Excuse me, madam,' the star said humbly, 'but I am a pedlar.'

'I don't want anything.'

'Everyone in the world needs what I am selling.'

'What's that?'

'I sell Virtue.'

'If you sell Virtue shouldn't you buy it too?'

'Of course, but why do you ask?'

'Because I have some to sell,' the old maid answered.

'Let me see it. Perhaps we can do some business.'

12

Then the woman brought a piece of Virtue from a cupboard. But it was old and patched, and so full of tears, so stained and moth-eaten, that the star could not tell what it had been like when it was new, all of twenty years ago.

'How much will you give me if I will sell it to you?' asked the woman.

'How much will you give me if I buy it from you?' answered the star.

'You impertinent creature!' the woman shouted, tearing the piece of stuff away from second star.

But the poor stuff was so tattered and easily torn that it fell to pieces as if it had been a spider's web. It was a sorry business, for the old maid threatened to go to law and have the poor star punished for saying that her virtue was worthless; and the little pedlar ran the risk of being fined or even put in prison. So she offered to give the woman a nice new piece to replace the worn out one.

The woman made the star turn out her whole box-full of goods. But although it contained all manner of virtues her grumbling customer could find nothing to suit her fancy.

And so second star was forced to offer her money instead, and after long bargaining the sum was fixed at five francs. The star took from her pocket a new ten franc coin and politely asked her for five francs change. The old woman left the room pretending to go and get the money, but came back with a policeman.

'Here's the young woman who stole into my house to rob me,' she said. 'Arrest her and take her to prison.'

It was in vain that second star pleaded her innocence, and repeated that she was waiting for her change. The constable, who came from the provinces, did not understand very clearly what the old woman had told him, so he told the seller of Virtue that she must come with him to the police-station. The star could do nothing else but obey.

As she was marched along the two or three streets leading

13

from the old maid's house to the police-station all the little street-boys ran at her heels calling out: 'Thief! Thief!'

When she was taken into the presence of the sergeant the little star told her tale so simply and quietly that that good man who, thanks to a sharp eye knew many things that nobody else guessed, sent the constable away and when he was left alone with his prisoner asked how she earned her living.

The star opened her box and showed him her wares. The sergeant burst out laughing. 'My dear child,' he said, 'yours is a trade that's no good at all, and if you have no other way of making a living I must ask you to leave the city. It has enough poor already.'

The poor little star hung her head and made her way out of the city leaving her box with the sergeant who, at a dinner given to his men on the following Christmas Day, gave its contents away as presents.

And that is why, ever since then, most policemen have always been so very kind and helpful.

On that same day the third star also entered the very same city. She was the one given the command to sell Health.

'Health! Health for sale!' she cried. 'Who lacks Health?'

'What! You're selling health?' people on all sides called out when they heard her.

'Yes. Health for sale! Health for sale! Who'll buy?'

In the twinkling of an eye she was surrounded by a large crowd. Everyone wanted health, everyone clamoured for it, until the stage was reached when the poor star didn't know who to listen to first. But most of those who stretched out eager hands for the magic cure had long ago ruined their own health and had chased it from their bodies. Health, which has its own pride, never particularly cares to return to places where it has been treated with such disdain.

Others asked the star: 'Does it cost much to keep your health?'

'Oh, good heavens, no,' she replied.

'What does it eat? What does it drink? How must we look after it?'

And the little pedlar answered: 'It eats not too much and not too little. It drinks pure clear water, goes to bed early and gets up with the sun.'

At this the crowd turned up their noses, and said: 'It's perfectly clear that this girl has no idea of how to sell her wares. One might just as well become a hermit to try to keep your health.'

But there were two kinds of people in the crowd who muttered to themselves:

'If by any bad luck this health-seller should make a fortune we are ruined.' These were the doctors and the grave-diggers.

I have said 'two kinds of people,' but I ought to have said only one, for in this city the doctors and the grave-diggers had joined together and started in business as 'Messrs Death and Company'. So they clustered together and talked the matter over, in the end making up their minds to rid the city of this strange pedlar and her wares, cost what it may.

The grave-diggers were to see to the wares, while the doctors were to take charge of the pedlar. So, on the sly, one of the grave-diggers grabbed the box and ran off with it.

The unfortunate little star ran after him, crying: 'Stop thief! Stop thief! He has stolen my Health!'

A doctor hurried to catch up with her and when he had reached her said in a soothing voice: 'Come with me, my dear, come with me. Your box will be returned to you.'

Third star looked at him, and seeing that he was well-dressed, although looking rather glum, she took him at his word and followed him. He took her to a hospital.

When the poor star realised where she had been brought she tried to get out as quickly as she could, but the door was closed on her. She saw that she had been caught in a trap.

'Oh, doctor, doctor!' she cried, 'have pity on me and let me out. I am quite well.'

'You are wrong?' he answered, 'you are very ill.'

'But I eat well.'

'Bad sign.'

'I drink well.'

'Bad sign.'

'I sleep well.'

'Bad sign.'

'I have clear eyes, an even pulse, a clean pink tongue . . .'

'Bad sign. Bad sign. Bad sign.'

As the star kept on saying that she was quite well and would not go to bed the learned man left her with two nurses who undressed little third star in spite of herself, and tied her down in bed.

'Aha,' said the doctor when he returned, 'so you'll interfere with us by selling good health when we sell ill-health, will you? Instead of joining us you want to work against us, do you? You'll see, you'll see, my fine friend.'

And he sent for three other doctors and they held what they called a 'consultation', and what their allies, the grave-diggers, called 'a sentence of death'. They decided that she should have what they described as a 'special kind of treatment' which would work quickly.

First, they put her on a special diet. Then they bled her every day. Finally, under the pretext that she slept too much they tickled the soles of her feet every time the star closed her eyes.

Luckily, she was a star, this little seller of Health and, therefore, immortal. She did not die, because she couldn't, but she was very, very ill. Luckily, again, the keeper whose duty it was to keep an eye on her fell asleep one night. The tiny patient managed first to free one of her arm-rays and then the other, then one of the leg-rays and then the other. At last she slipped quietly out of bed, opened a window, tied a sheet to the bars, wrapped herself in another, and slid down into the hospital garden.

The garden was enclosed by walls, but all along one side climbing fruit trees were trained and the little creature scrambled up the wall with their help. Once outside that terrifying place the star set off running as fast as she possibly could.

The hospital and the cemetery were next door to each other, so that everyone who passed by thought that she must have come not from the hospital but from the cemetery. Instead of taking her for an escaped invalid they believed that she was a ghost risen from the dead. Indeed, the sheet with which she had covered herself made her look even more like a ghost. So, instead of running after her and stopping her, everybody in the street, even including the sentry who stood at the gates of the city, shrank from her and let her pass.

'Oh,' she said to herself, 'if Jupiter has another box-full of Health to send to the earth he can find some other messenger.'

Now I, being the recorder of these wonderful adventures, have made enquiries and found out that the grave-digger who stole the box of Health from the star took it to his comrades, telling them what was inside. Then all of them set to work to dig an enormous hole in the form of a ditch in the cemetery, threw all the Health into it, and filled it up again.

So no one but the dead profited by Jupiter's good intentions, for it is ever since then that the dead have been so well.

While the star of Health was being coaxed by trickery into the hospital, where most certainly she would have died if she had not been immortal, someone in another part of the city was calling out her wares, but with no greater success. This was the fourth star who was trying to do good business, and was shouting:

'Who wishes for a Long Life? Who wants to live for ever? Buy as many years as you like! Buy! Buy!'

At the sound of her voice the whole city seemed to be turned topsy-turvy.

A wealthy banker who had houses in Paris, Frankfurt, New

17

York, Vienna and London, ordered his agent to raise as many millions as were needed to buy the box and all its contents for him alone.

The lords of the manor begged that the star should be closely guarded in case the ordinary people should be able to buy any of the precious stuff. The bishops and all the rest of the clergy hurried to meet and consult together about the matter. As a result the archbishop telegraphed to the Pope, who replied:

'Those who buy Long Life should pay tithes, a year for every ten years they buy.'

Parliament ordered that everybody who bought Long Life should pay a special tax.

The banker came along with his millions to buy up the star's whole stock, but there was a riot with shouts of 'Fair shares for all!', and they beat him up and very nearly killed him.

Then the king, who was a good king, forbade the tax that parliament had ordered and commanded that Long Life should be sold openly and that all, except those condemned to death, should have the right to buy, each according to his means. Immediately everyone crowded round the star, one hand full of gold and the other empty:

'Long Life! Long Life! Here's my money, take my money – oh, *please*, do take my money!' everybody begged her.

'Long Life to *me* please – to *me*, ME, ME!'

'All in good time, ladies and gentlemen,' the star answered, 'but have you bought the goods which my three sisters were selling?'

'What were they selling?' was asked in chorus, the buyers eager to get the precious ware from the star's box.

'The first was Wit.'

'We haven't bought any.'

'The second sold Virtue.'

'Nor any of that either.'

'The third sold Health.'

'We know nothing about the sale.'

18

'Then,' replied the seller of Long Life, 'I am very sorry, but without Wit, Virtue and Health, Long Life would be of no use to you.' And she closed her box, refusing to sell her wares to those who hadn't had the sense to buy what her three sisters had offered to sell.

But when she had packed up the star found that she had overlooked one little piece of Long Life – a sample of her goods. It was a scrap that gave three hundred years of life. Close by her a parrot was sitting on its perch.

'Have you had your breakfast, Jacquot,' she asked.

'No, Margot,' the bird replied.

The star laughed. She gave him the piece of Long Life she was holding. The parrot ate it to the last crumb.

And that is why parrots live such a long, long time.

While the seller of Long Life was watching the bird gobbling up its strange meal she heard a great noise in the crowd.

'Honour! Honour! Who'll buy Honour?'

It was, of course, the fifth star who had entered the city.

All the people who had refused to buy Wit, Virtue and Health, and who had been refused Long Life because of that, started an uproar. At the cry of 'Honour!' 'Honour!' they had made up their minds not to buy any of the new wares but to get hold of them, if they could, for nothing and by any means possible. So they rushed at the unlucky fifth star who, finding herself threatened, opened her box and shook it.

A thousand things fell out – titles, crosses of honour, ribbons, gold watches, epaulettes, and so on. Every single person in the crowd fell upon one or the other of these prizes and rushed away, each thinking that he was carrying off Honour when, of course, the clever little star had only shaken out 'honours'. Which is not the same thing at all.

The real, the true, Honour stayed at the bottom of the star's box, just as Hope was left in Pandora's Box.

And that is why Honour is so rarely found, and why honours are so common.

While all this was happening the sixth star came on the scene calling: 'Pleasure! Who'll buy Pleasure?'

All who heard the call ran after her. Even those who had got their full share of honours wanted to find out what these new goods were like. So all of them, with crosses on their breasts, titles in their pockets, ribbons about their necks, gold watches on their chains, and epaulettes on their shoulders, hurried with the others to get their turn at pleasure also.

But all the others cried out angrily that these men wanted too many of the good things of life, and they called them, among other rude things, greedy. Soon there was another riot. Someone tore the box of wares from the star's grasp, then, again, others snatched it away from whoever was holding it.

In the middle of all this hullabaloo the box fell on the pavement and broke into pieces. Pleasures were scattered over the road in every direction, and one and all scrambled madly for them. So that it happened that not each got hold of the pleasure he wanted and which he thought suited him; but, in fact, each got his neighbour's pleasure so, although they all had a share of the goods it was all very much of a lottery.

That old rogue, Chance, had great delight by mocking the poor wretches with his gifts; to the women he gave the manly pleasure of the chase and hunting, to the men laces and ribbons, to the gouty a love of dancing, to the deaf a liking for listening to music, to the blind a love of painting and sculptures, to the old men calf-love, and to the old women sisterly love.

In short, he gave to no one what he wanted to have, and so no-one was happy and everyone cursed the poor little pedlar. The result was that the star took to her heels and hurried out of the town without being paid.

Ever since then the pleasures of life have been so badly shared out among mankind that we look upon a man as a fool if he lives for pleasure alone.

As soon as the unfortunate seller of Pleasure, who had been

so shamefully robbed of her wares, had left the city she came across her seventh sister who, you may remember, was to sell Riches lying senseless in a ditch by the side of the road.

The star of Pleasure ran to her and threw herself down by the girl. She took the poor star's head upon her knees and made her sniff some smelling-salts which luckily she had with her. But it was only after some time that the seventh star recovered her senses.

As soon as she was well enough to talk she told her story, and it was this:

'Scarcely had I come within sight of the city, scarcely had I been silly enough to tell the people what I was selling, scarcely had they learned that I was laden with Riches, than they all fell upon me, robbed me, and left me for dead, as you have seen.'

'But who were these dreadful people?' asked the other five stars who had just joined the pair. 'Thieves? Paupers? Starving men?'

'Oh, no! They were millionaires, my dear sisters,' sighed the seventh star.

When the seven stars had flown back to Olympus and told their master of the way they had been treated on earth Jupiter scowled a terrible scowl.

But Neptune and Pluto burst out laughing. 'What did we tell you, your majesty,' they cried. 'It was such a comical thought!' And they repeated, both together as in a duet: 'Oh, it was such an odd idea!'

In the end Jupiter reluctantly had to agree with them.

And this, word for word, is the story found by the gaoler in the table-drawer of the prisoner's cell in the king-poet's capital.

THE PHANTOM WHITE HARE

First of all I must tell you that this story was told to me by an innkeeper whose grandfather was an apothecary, or what is known today as a chemist. He lived in a village called Theux not far from Liége, and as his grandfather was an only son he had been left a good business as well as some thousands of francs which had, in fact, been made by buying herbs for less than nothing and selling them for a great deal. Indeed it could be said that his grandfather was more of a herbalist than an apothecary. He would certainly have been much richer but for two reasons – he was a hunter and a scholar.

As a result of all his reading the old man doubted everything, even the saints, even God. He forbade his wife to go to mass on any other day than Sunday, and gave her permission to mention in her prayers whoever she wished except himself. Moreover, he would not allow her and their children to kneel at night around her bed and pray together, as, since time immemorial it had been the custom for the family to do. As time went on they were no longer allowed, when the bell for extreme unction was heard, to go out and accompany the Holy Sacrament to the home of one of the faithful who was dying.

It is true that he was so often absent hunting, leaving so early and returning so late, especially on Sundays, that his wife was perfectly free on these days not only to hear mass, but even high mass, vespers and evening prayers and, on other days, to follow the Holy Sacrament wherever it went. To such acquaintances as she met in the church or in the house of the dying she said:

'Do not tell Jerome that you have seen me.'

These absences, which were gradually extended from Sundays to other days of the week, gave his wife every opportunity for remaining a good Christian in spite of her husband's orders.

At first Jerome had devoted only Sundays to hunting and, so far, provided he did not trespass on the lands of the prince-bishop or those of the lords of the manor of Theux and its neighbourhood, no one could complain and, in fact, no one did. But he soon reasoned that it was not too much, since he remained seated in his shop the other six days of the week, for him to give himself a little further distraction not only on Sundays but also on Thursdays. Then followed Tuesday, and finally the other days as though drawn in the train of the first. There thus came a time when instead of one day when Jerome would go out hunting, and six during which he would stay at home, it became the reverse. Eventually the seventh day also ended by going the way of the others! So thus he more and more withdrew himself from his wife and children.

Not only did he spend his days in the woods, the fields and the marshes, braving rain, storms and snow; in the evenings, instead of returning home to warm himself beside the fire and eat with his family, he would spend his time drinking at the inn with companions and telling of his prowess to the first-comer. He told at one and the same time his deeds of yesterday, of today, and even those which he contemplated tomorrow.

These evenings, drowned first in beer, then in local wine, then in Rhine wines, became prolonged to such an extent that it often happened he did not return home at all. He left at daybreak the next day, sometimes even earlier, from the inn in which he had spent the previous night. The result was that Jerome hunted so often and so much that the game became scarce on the lands and in the woods of the public property on which he had the perfect right to shoot, as well as on the private lands where he was tolerated.

Thus, gradually, he intruded onto the property of the prince-bishop and others. They were at first timid excursions which he kept within reason, lying in wait at points just over the borders, and in other similar trifling ways. But in the times when Jerome lived even this was risky. Justice did not laugh at hunting offences; the lords of the manor were still all-powerful, and they decided on the sentence and would without hesitation send a poor devil to the galleys for a rabbit.

When, very rarely, he did stay at home in the evenings Jerome was a 'bon vivant'; he always had in his cellar in addition to a cask of good Brussels beer a barrel of Rhine wine, and, on the table beside his full glass an empty one which only awaited a visit from a friend for it to be filled. As he was never happier than when any of the foresters came to sit beside him under the high chimney-piece and clink glasses with him as they chattered over details of the chase they were neither hard nor severe on him. As often as they could these foresters shut their eyes to his peccadillos, and when they heard his gun fired or his dogs barking in one direction they moved away in the other.

But there is no rule without its exceptions, and there was one in this case among the foresters. His name was Thomas Pihay, and he hated Jerome. While they were still children they could never bear each other. Thomas was rather fat, thick-set and had red hair. Jerome was tall, dark and thin. Thomas had a slight squint and was not particularly good-looking, while Jerome had perfectly straight eyes and was rather handsome. All these circumstances, as well as a number of others, had caused a real hatred between the two of them.

In the end Thomas left the district to go to work as a forester in Luxembourg, but unfortunately his master died. It was, for Jerome, a piece of bad luck that a friend of Thomas wrote to him that there was a job for him on the prince-bishop's estates, so he returned to Theux and Jerome and Thomas found themselves neighbours.

Hearing from everybody that Jerome had become as great a

hunter before God as Nimrod, and that because of his passion for the chase he almost always shut his eyes when he found himself facing ditches and other landmarks which showed the limits of public property and private lands, Thomas promised himself at the first opportunity given to him to prove that if two mountains cannot meet then two men can.

Jerome was now aware of this fresh animosity when he learned of Pihay's return. He was very annoyed then, for he was really a good-hearted man, and when on the first occasion as he was sitting at a table with a good bottle of wine beside him he saw Thomas Pihay pass he got up and went to the door, and called out:

'Hallo, Thomas.'

Pihay turned round and, pale as death, asked:

'What do you want?'

Jerome had gone in, filled two glasses, and returning to the door with a glass in each hand, said: 'Come and have a drink with me.'

Thomas shook his head, 'Not with you Jerome', and continued on his way.

Jerome went back to where he had been sitting and drank both glasses, one after the other, shaking his head in turn, and muttering to himself: 'This will end badly, Thomas, of that I'm sure.'

He little thought how truly he spoke.

I am sure you will understand that with such animosity between two men, particularly with one an obsessed hunter and the other a forester, a catastrophe was bound to follow sooner or later. That was everyone's opinion, and it happened sooner than was expected.

Jerome, by now, was no longer content with penetrating just over the boundaries of all these private lands when his dogs led him there. He was going further afield, finding not only a mischievous pleasure in braving simultaneously the spiritual and temporal authority of the prince-bishop, but even a double pleasure in doing so. You will know, by now, that matters could not continue for very long like this.

One day monseigneur was stag-hunting with some young lords and ladies – the prince-bishops of Liége were always very gallant princes – and in spite of the fine company he was in a bad mood. This was justified, for three times during the morning his dogs had gone on a wrong scent. They were finally called off and the prince-bishop, who had promised his guests that they would be in at the death, was furious.

But suddenly at the moment when they were starting to return to the bishop's palace a magnificent stag crossed at a bound the end of a glade.

'By Saint Hubert!' the bishop shouted, and then called out to one of the foresters: 'See if its tracks are the same as those of the one we lost earlier.'

The forester bent over the animal's tracks.

'Good heavens, yes, monseigneur,' he said, 'they are the very same.'

'Are you sure?'

'Absolutely sure. I had already told your grace that the stag had one hoof worn to the heel. Look.'

The prince-bishop leaned from his horse to examine the trail. It was the very same. Suddenly he lifted his head and listened, and then said: 'That stag is being hunted.'

In fact, the slight breeze began to bring to the company of hunters the noise of distant barking. Somebody remarked that the barking must be coming from their own dogs somewhere in the distance.

'Nonsense,' the prince-bishop replied, 'they are someone else's dogs, and what is more they are following that stag.'

They all listened and looked at one another.

'Yes, you are right, they are dogs in full cry,' one of the foresters said.

'Whose dogs are they?' asked the prince-bishop, pale with rage.

No one said a word.

'By Saint Hubert,' the bishop went on, 'I want to know who is hunting on my land. But we'll soon see. Where the stag has passed the dogs will follow.'

Nobody moved. They all waited.

But you will have guessed that the dogs hunting the stag, of which the prince-bishop's dogs had lost the scent, were those of Jerome.

2

You should, I think, know something about Jerome's dogs.

They were admirable dogs, magnificent beasts, each worth its weight in gold, with jet black coats, breasts and bellies the colour of flame, hair dry and rough as a wolf's, long feet, lean and gaunt. Dogs that could hunt hare, deer or stags for eight or ten hours at a stretch, enjoying themselves, never losing the scent, and when the trail is fresh staying together with only inches separating them.

They soon showed up and without taking the slightest heed of the prince-bishop, his party or his pack, sprang from the undergrowth, scented the spot where the stag had put his feet, and pushed into the brushwood opposite redoubling their barking.

'Whose brutes are those?' monseigneur shouted.

The foresters stayed silent as though they knew neither the dogs nor their master. Unfortunately Thomas Pihay was near. He thought the moment good for satisfying some of his hatred for Jerome and getting into the good books of his new employer.

'They belong to Jerome Palan, the apothecary in Theux, monseigneur,' he answered.

'Have the dogs killed,' the prince-bishop said, 'and their owner arrested.'

The order was clear and there could be no misunderstanding.

'Fine!' Pihay said to the other foresters, 'you look after Palan and I will attend to the dogs.'

Although it would be with lumps in their throats when they arrested Jerome they preferred to do this than the deed Pihay had reserved for himself. In fact, no one who knew Jerome could forget that he would bear a very different grudge against anyone who shot his dogs than he would have for those who arrested him.

So while Thomas Pihay thrust himself into a thicket on the left, going as fast as he could in the direction taken by the dogs of his enemy, the others turned and pushed through the brushwood on the right. When they were out of sight of the prince-bishop the five of them stopped to discuss what they should do. Three were bachelors; two were married. The three single men were inclined to warn Jerome instead of arresting him. Jerome would be certain to make for the open, and they could say that they had not seen him and that, doubtless, the dogs had escaped from their kennels and were hunting alone. But the two married men shook their heads.

'Well, why not?' asked the others.

'If the prince-bishop found out not only would we lose our jobs but something worse might happen.'

'Look, it is better to risk losing our jobs and even go to prison than to arrest a good friend like Jerome Palan,' one of the single men said.

'We have wives and children,' objected the married men.

There was no answer to that – the safety of wives and families went before that of strangers, and the married men carried the day.

It was not difficult to find Jerome, for he always followed his dogs as closely as possible, finding, he said, a better opportunity of firing effectively in this way than by preceding them. The foresters had gone only a few yards further when they came upon him and to their great regret, single men as well as married, seized and disarmed him, pinioned him, and then led him to Liége.

In the meantime Thomas Pihay had hurried on his way, like a man to whom the devil had whispered bad counsel. Different from Jerome he had decided to go ahead of the dogs, and guided by their baying he stood on the slope of a small hill with a windmill on its top. He recognised the track of the stag, for the trail was a well-known one, and he had no doubts that the dogs, too, would follow it. He crouched behind a hedge.

The noise of the dogs came nearer. Never when lying in wait for any game had Pihay's heart beat faster. The dogs appeared. He aimed at the leading one, and fired. With the first shot he brought down Flambeau; with the second, Ramette. Flambeau was Jerome's best dog, and Ramette was a bitch. The remaining two dogs were named Ramoneau and Spiron. Pihay had quite deliberately killed Ramette in preference to any of the others so that Jerome could never breed from her. This done he left the two dogs stretched dead on the ground and while Ramoneau and Spiron continued to follow the stag he went home.

Jerome and his guards chatted away on the road to Liége like good friends returning to town after a pleasant walk in the woods. Jerome seemed quite unaware of his predicament and appeared only preoccupied about his dogs and the stag they were hunting.

'My word,' he said to the forester Jonas Deshayes who was walking on his left, 'that was a splendid beast and certainly one that would tempt any hunter.'

'Yes, but I wish to goodness you had decided on some other day than this, Monsieur Palan,' Jonas answered. 'Why on earth did you stick your neck out like this? Didn't you hear our dogs?'

'Of course. But they follow so badly that I took them for shepherd's dogs rounding up a flock. Listen! See what I call good hunting!'

And Jerome stopped, enchanted by the sound of his dogs which were chasing the stag magnificently.

'But how did it all come about?' asked the forester on his right, Luc Thévelin.

'This is what happened. My dogs were chasing a hare. I waited, squatting in a ditch. Suddenly I saw your stag appear. About a hundred feet away from me he went into a thicket, and ten minutes later I saw it come out driving before it a much younger deer which it forced to take its place in front of your dogs. That stag of yours knows all the tricks and it seemed amusing to me not to allow the rascal to enjoy the fruits of its trick. So I called back my dogs and put them on its trail. Do you know, Thévelin, that they have been hunting that stag for all of three hours? Can you hear them?'

'Agreed that they are the best dogs round here, but all the same this is going to be a very bad business for you Monsieur Palan.'

Jerome, however, was not listening – he was paying heed to his dogs. Forgetting that he was a prisoner he was rubbing his hands together and whistling with all the strength of his lungs to encourage them. At that very moment he heard two gunshots.

'Listen,' he said, 'there are your hunters who have not had the patience to be in at the death and have shot the stag.' Then, as barking could still be heard he added: 'I wonder who was the duffer who fired and missed. Next time he should aim at an elephant.'

The foresters exchanged anxious looks for they knew who had fired those two shots. Suddenly Jerome's expression altered and he became serious.

'Luc, Jonas, how many dogs can you hear?'

'I don't know,' they replied together.

'Listen! I can hear only two, Ramoneau and Spiron. What has happened to Flambeau and Ramette?'

'You are confusing the two with the other pack.'

'Me? I know the voices of my dogs, and only Ramoneau and Spiron are after that stag.'

'Look, Monsieur Palan,' Jonas replied, 'what do you think could have happened to your dogs? Flambeau and Ramette have either stopped or gone after some hare which diverted them.'

'My dogs,' said Jerome, 'stop only when I tell them to. They don't go after a hare when hunting a stag, even if the hare not only leapt into their sight but into their mouths.'

Poor Jerome, so happy a few minutes ago, now felt almost ready to weep. Every ten steps he stopped and listened. Then in true desolation: 'You are right. There are only Spiron and Ramoneau. But what has happened to the others, tell me, I implore you.'

The foresters did their best to console and comfort him. They tried to persuade him that the two dogs had returned home. But he didn't bother even to answer, only shaking his head and saying to himself between sighs: 'Something has happened to them.'

In this way the long walk to Liége was made, and Jerome was handed over to the police. He was flung into a cell about eight feet square and the door was closed on him with a loud clang of bolts. But the shock of finding himself in such a place would certainly have worried him less if he had been reassured as to the fate of Flambeau and Ramette.

Jerome woke next day still thinking of his two favourite dogs. Used to an active open-air life he could not bear the isolation of imprisonment. In vain he stood on a stool to breathe through the bars the air borne to him on the wind from the Ardennes; in vain he gazed at the horizon far beyond the Meuse, which circled the town like a silver ribbon, at his beloved woods of Theux. He transported himself there in his imagination, recalling the scents, the little cascades of light which came through the foliage, the confused noise of branches swaying in a breeze and murmuring in the night. Then, Jerome, suddenly finding

31

himself again in his cold, bare cell, with grey, damp walls fell into utter despair and grieved so much that he fell ill.

A doctor was allowed to visit him. The doctor, perhaps naturally enough, took a greater interest in the case of a patient who was an apothecary. He arranged for him to be given a less depressing cell, more food than he had been getting, and promised to bring him some books. At the same time he undertook to see if the prince-bishop would agree to him being let off with a heavy fine if the money to pay it could be found.

After a month's captivity Jerome learned from the doctor that his wife had also begged the burgomaster and magistrate of Theux to make the same request, and that the prince-bishop had agreed that on payment of ten thousand florins he would be set free at once. This sum comprised almost the whole of the family savings, but the good news filled Jerome with so much happiness that he could not close his eyes all night – he was going to see his home again, to find once more his big armchair close to the hearth, his gun hanging by the chimney, that excellent gun with which he so rarely missed aim; he was going to the welcoming greeting of his dogs, which, all four, he was counting on finding again for he had reached the same conclusion as Luc and Jonas that Flambeau and Ramette must have followed another animal's scent. Finally, he remembered also, and this was not his smallest joy, that he was going to be able to hold his wife and children in his arms.

Cheerful as his hopes were they did not stop Jerome from finding the time dragging so, to shorten it, he had what proved the fatal idea of taking from their hiding-place one of the books lent to him by the doctor. Having lit his little lamp he started to read. Ill luck would have it, however, that though the book was interesting he fell asleep, and so deep a sleep that a turnkey seeing the light glowing entered quietly and took away the volume without waking him.

The turnkey couldn't read, which was unfortunate. He handed the book to the prince-bishop's treasurer, who found the matter serious. He passed the volume over to the prince-bishop who, by merely inspecting the title, promptly flung the book into the fire, and decided at once that the apothecary of Theux should pay a double fine, half for his crime of hunting and half for his anti-Christian reading. This meant not only the sacrifice of Jerome's savings but also that of his business. He would need to sell the pharmacy, and that would take time.

So Jerome still stayed in prison and, since the irreligious reader had been caught in the very act, he had been returned to his former cell. But one day the bolts of his cell screeched, the massive door turned on its hinges, and his wife fell into Jerome's arms.

'At last! At last!' she cried out, covering her husband's haggard face with kisses, 'you are free, poor Jerome, even though we are hopelessly ruined.'

'Bah! Even if we are ruined I will work,' Jerome replied. 'This fortune I have lost, well, I'll build it up again. But let's get out of here, I'm suffocating.'

Together they went to monseigneur's treasurer who counted out the money, and during the whole time poor Jerome could not stop himself from looking at it from the corners of his eyes. Then he listened, trembling with rage, to the little lecture with which the priest judged it fitting to accompany the receipt for the fine. As soon as the receipt was in his hands, taking his wife's arm, he hurried to leave the prison and the town.

When they reached the road his wife, without reproaching her husband, spoke a good deal of their destitution; it was clear that she wanted Jerome to arrive home thoroughly aware of the seriousness of their situation and to no longer spend so large a part of his time in the costly sport of hunting. But Jerome, the closer they came to Theux, paid less and less notice to what his wife was saying – indeed, so preoccupied was he that he seemed to scarcely listen. On breathing the air of the streets the anxieties that he had left in the prison came back to him again.

Yet, worried as he was, he did not once ask his wife for news of the dogs.

As he entered the house he did not even glance at his empty pharmacy or deserted laboratory. He kissed his two children and then went straight to the kennels. A moment later he returned wild-eyed and with a face as pale as death.

'My dogs!' he cried. 'Where are my dogs? Where are they? Have you sold them to add to the money-bags of that wretched bishop? Are they dead? Answer me.'

'Which dogs?' his wife asked, trembling.

'Why, Flambeau and Ramette.'

'They were killed, father,' one of the children answered.

'Killed! And who killed them?'

The child did not speak, but his wife answered: 'I thought you knew that monseigneur ordered your dogs to be shot.'

Jerome became livid. 'He ordered that? Who dared to obey?' And suddenly a light flashed through his mind. 'There is only one man, only one in the world, who could have committed such a crime. It was Thomas Pihay.'

'Since then everyone in the town shuns him like the plague,' his wife said.

'As for the bishop I don't know who will avenge me on him,' Jerome shouted, 'but Thomas Pihay – I will settle his account just as truly as I don't believe in God.'

His wife trembled from head to foot, less at the threat than at the blasphemy.

'Dear Jerome, don't ever say such a thing if you do not wish to make yourself, your wife, and your children accursed.'

Jerome didn't reply. He sat down thoughtfully in his usual chair. He ate his supper without asking anything about what had happened. Next day, as he had promised his wife, he went about seeking work. He had no difficulty in finding it and was well paid for what he did. Comfort began once more to gradually return to the house.

3

Jerome's character changed. He became as sad and morose as he had once been cheerful and carefree. He never laughed, and hardly spoke to anyone. Often, for no reason, he would suddenly burst into violent and bitter words against the world in general and his neighbours in particular with the result that, little by little, these neighbours drew away from him.

As for his irreligion, it had increased. Formerly it had scarcely been evident except in jokes, and songs sung at hunting evenings. But now the very sight of a cassock infuriated him and if he passed before a crucifix, and because it was hot was carrying his hat, he made a show of putting it back on his head. Not only did he pour forth invectives against all priests, but also against all divine faith which he blasphemously attacked.

What specially saddened his wife was that since his return she had not once been to mass. To be sure she told the children when they went to or came back from school, or even when they went out to play, to go into the church and pray for themselves, for her, and above all for their father. It is true that as soon as she was alone in the house or by herself in her room she repeated all the prayers she knew. But she kept wondering whether these prayers were worth as much as those she would have said in church. And so she wept a lot, which exasperated Jerome almost as much as the sight of a priest's black robe did.

One day when he found her crying Jerome said: 'What's the matter? I work, don't I? You lack for nothing and neither do the children. I don't go hunting any more, in fact I have never touched my gun or let loose my dogs since I came home.'

'I know all that, Jerome, I know all that.'

'What is it then? What do you want? Tell me, I won't eat you.'

'Well,' the poor woman replied, 'I wish you wouldn't make enemies of all your friends. I wish you would be a little happier, and go hunting, not every day the Lord forbid, but on holidays and Sundays. I wish, and this is what I most wish, that you would no longer curse God and His church, my dear Jerome.'

'As for my friends,' Jerome replied, 'they turn their backs on *me* because none of them want the friendship of a poor man. And as for being happy, any joy that I had was killed six months ago and nothing can, or will, revive it.'

'But . . . .' murmured his wife. She did not finish.

'Yes, I understand,' said Jerome gloomily, 'you don't like the way I speak of God and his saints. Well, if the way I speak of them annoys them let them show their anger.'

His wife was frightened, but she managed to say: 'In the old days there was at least one saint you were devoted to.'

'No, I don't remember.'

'Saint Hubert, the patron of hunting.'

'Yes, I liked him, and I never failed to drink his health at those good dinners for which he served as a good excuse to give.' And with a little smile: 'But he always forgot to ask for the bill! So I have broken with him.' Then, impatiently, he went on: 'Let us stop joking. I love you and the children, but I have no need to love anyone else. I work hard to make your life comfortable, and I will go on doing so, but on one condition.'

'What is that?'

'That you leave my conscience in peace.'

There was nothing to say to this for she knew Jerome only too well.

Later when his children came in Jerome took them on his knees and jogged them in imitation of a horse. His wife gazed at him in astonishment. Not for six months had she seen such a thing happening.

'Wife,' he said, 'tomorrow is Sunday, the day for hunting as you said a while ago. Well, on this point at least, you will see me follow your advice. As for gaiety let's hope that will come back in its turn.' And he rubbed his hands. 'You see, I am growing more cheerful. I think I will have a drink for it's a long time since I had one.'

His wife brought him a little glass, like those from which liqueurs are drunk.

'What is that?' Jerome cried out. 'Give me a wine-glass. I want to make up for lost time.'

As his wife hesitated, he put the children down and went to look for a glass to his liking. Then he held it out and at his request his wife filled it three times in succession.

'Not only is tomorrow Sunday,' Jerome said as he drank, 'but it is also Saint Hubert's feast-day. So I toast the health of the saint, to his eternal glory in the world of hunting and we will wait and see what game he produces. Whatever I shoot I will not sell. We will all eat it together. Now, children what would you like?'

'I,' said the boy, 'I would like a hare, with all that lovely gravy mother knows so well how to make.'

'Me too,' said the little girl, 'it's so long since we have eaten one.'

'Well you shall have your hare,' and Jerome looked lovingly at his gun hanging over the mantel-piece. 'You hear great Saint Hubert? A hare! I must have one even if I have to shoot it between your feet.'

In fact, above the gun was a painting of Saint Hubert with a hare taking refuge between his feet.

Next day at sunrise Jerome set out with Ramoneau and Spiron. Although it was very early in November the ground was covered with snow. The dogs sank up to their chests in it and couldn't run. Moreover, the hares had not left their hides and so there were no traces for him to follow. Jerome beat the country for most of the day but, skilful as he was, could find nothing and returned home with an empty game-bag. But he was still in a good humour, and after supper he went to shut up the dogs, took down his gun again, and kissed his wife and children.

'What are you going to do?' asked his wife, who was quite astonished.

'I am going to lie in wait. Didn't I promise the children a hare?'

'You will get one next Sunday, Jerome.'

'I promised it to them today and not next Sunday. It would be a nice thing if I were to break my word.'

'Yes, a hare as big as Ramoneau,' the boy said, laughing.

'Be easy,' said Jerome, 'you will have your hare. They will be about tonight, and in the moonlight I'll see them on the snow as big as elephants.'

Jerome went out, his gun on his shoulder. As he left he was whistling the same tune as he had done on the day when Thomas Pihay had killed two of his dogs. He thought that, the snow still falling, the hares would go to the hollows and so he went to station himself in a valley at the cross-roads between two villages. The place was well-chosen for there were bushes behind which he could shelter and hide. He had been there nearly a quarter of an hour when he heard someone approaching singing.

'The devil!' Jerome exclaimed, 'here comes a rascal who is going to scare away my hare if it's anywhere near.'

The voice came nearer and nearer. The sound of the snow crackling under the feet of the singer soon distinctly reached the ears of Jerome who did not stir from his hiding-place. The moon was at the full and its reflection from the snow covering the ground made its light all the stronger. Soon Jerome was almost certain that the man who was approaching was Thomas Pihay. He held his breath, but when he was quite sure that it was the murderer of Flambeau and Ramette who was about to pass near his ambush his heart started to beat as if it would burst his ribs, and his fingers convulsively gripped the barrel and stock of his gun.

At bottom, however, Jerome was not an evil man and he was certainly not bad-hearted. So he decided to let Pihay pass if he did not speak. Pihay did pass without speaking – he had not even seen Jerome. But by bad luck he took the same road by which Jerome had come and saw the footprints in the snow. He turned round, noticed the bushes, and suspected that someone was hiding behind them. Wondering who it could be he retraced his steps. Not wishing to give his enemy the satisfaction of catching him in his hiding-place Jerome rose to his feet. Pihay had not even thought of him and, doubtless remorseful for the evil thing he had done, seemed disconcerted.

'Well, Monsieur Palan,' he said in a voice as near affectionate as he could make it, 'here we are then in a hiding-place.'

Jerome didn't answer. He only wiped his forehead, which was covered with sweat, with the back of his sleeve.

'I wouldn't mind being where you are,' Pihay continued, 'for this north wind tonight is cold enough to redden the skin of a wolf.'

'Go away,' was all Jerome could find to say.

'Go away? Why should I? And by what right have you to order me?'

'Go away I tell you,' Jerome answered, striking the ground with the butt of his gun.

'Yes, now I understand. I must go away because you are in ambush, poaching, hunting in the snow.'

'Once more,' Jerome called out, 'the advice I give to you, Thomas Pihay, is to go away.'

Pihay hesitated for a moment, but no doubt he was ashamed to give in.

'No,' he said, 'I shall not just pass by and go on my way. When I recognised it was you I was on the point of leaving because since your imprisonment you have become crazy, and for madmen as for children one must have some indulgence. But, since you take that tone, I shall arrest you Monsieur Jerome Palan and show you a second time that I know how to carry out my duties.'

Then he walked straight towards Jerome.

'Thomas, not one step further . . . Thomas, don't provoke me!' Jerome said in an agitated voice.

'So you think you can frighten me, Jerome Palan,' Pihay replied, shaking his head. 'I am not as easily terrified as that.'

'Not another step I tell you!' shouted Jerome more threateningly. 'Already there is blood between us. Take care, or the snow will drink your blood as the earth did of my poor dogs.'

'Threats!' cried the forester. 'Do you think you can stop me with threats? It needs something a great deal more than that, and from a very different man, too, my friend.'

And raising his stick above his head he advanced further towards Jerome.

'You want it? You want it then?' Jerome bellowed. 'Well, let the blood that is going to flow recoil on the head of the one who is guilty.'

Jerome quickly raised his gun to his shoulder and fired both barrels together. There was only the sound of a single shot and, moreover, the noise was so faint that Jerome thought the priming alone had exploded – he had forgotten that snow deadened sound. So he seized his gun by the barrel to use it as a club. But suddenly he saw Pihay drop his stick, beat the air with his arms, spin round, and fall face down in the snow. Jerome's first movement was to run to him.

Thomas Pihay was dead, dying without a moan. The double discharge had passed through his chest. Jerome remained for some seconds standing mute, motionless. Then he remembered that Pihay had a wife and children awaiting his return. He imagined them anxious, hurrying to the door at the slightest noise, and he felt his hatred for Pihay disappear. Then it seemed to him that if he wished hard enough Pihay could be restored to life.

'Come, Thomas,' he said, 'come, Thomas, get up.'

There is no need for me to tell you that not only did the corpse not rise but there wasn't even one word of reply. Jerome stooped to take him under the arms to help him to rise, and only then, seeing the blood flowing and colouring the snow around him with a reddish circle, did he realise what he had done. His thoughts flew to his own wife and children. He wished to live, and yet to live he must conceal from all eyes this corpse which would bring upon him the vengeance of everyone. So he went back to his house, climbed a wall into the garden without waking anyone, took a pick and shovel, and returned with long strides to the crossroads.

As he went he was shaking with fear, as though he expected a judge and executioner to be waiting for him. When he was not more than a hundred yards away the moon, which had been hidden for some time, came out from the low and sombre clouds by which it had been shrouded, and brightly illuminated the white carpet of snow. All was silent, deserted, desolate.

Jerome glanced towards the cross-roads. An unheard of, an inexplicable thing, had happened. On the corpse an animal was sitting on its haunches, and from its long ears and its short front legs, Jerome saw that it was a hare.

Now Jerome was drenched with a cold sweat, and his hair rose on his head. He told himself that it was all his own imagination. He wanted to continue walking, but his feet seemed fixed to the ground. Yet moments were precious, for during Saint Hubert's night hunters would be numerous and some of them might pass and see the body. So he made a supreme effort, summoned all his courage to overcome his terror, and staggered forward like a drunken man.

What alarmed him further was that the hare, that most timid of animals, seemed to fear neither the dead nor the living and, what is more, it appeared to be three or four times larger than any ordinary hare. He remembered vaguely one of the children asking him to bring back a hare as big as Ramoneau. Was it, as in fairy tales, that the child's wish was to be granted?

Everything seemed so absurd that the thought came to him that he was dreaming, and he began to laugh. But an echo answered his laugh. It was the hare which also laughed, leaning back on its hind legs and holding its sides with its forepaws. Jerome stopped laughing. He shook himself, pinched himself, and looked at himself. Most certainly he was awake. He glanced back at the strange vision. It was still there – the body was lying on the snow and the hare was squatting on the body.

Now, I should tell you that the hare was covered with almost white fur and its eyes shone like those of a cat or a panther. Despite its appearance the certainty that he had to deal with a very inoffensive and ordinary animal calmed Jerome's terror. He felt sure that when it saw him come closer it would dash away. So he approached the body. The hare didn't budge. Jerome now touched the body with his foot, and still the hare did not make the slightest movement. But its eyes reflected more brightly the rays of the moon, and particularly so when they met those of Jerome.

He started to walk around the body and as he did so the hare pivoted, its eyes following him. Waving his arms Jerome shouted 'Brrrou! Brrrou!' which no hare would have ignored, were it the Alexander, the Hannibal or the Caesar of hares. But it was all useless, and Jerome's terror became greater than ever. He wanted to fling himself on his knees and pray, but all that happened was that his feet slipped and he fell forward on his hands. He got up again and tried at least to make the sign of the cross, but when he went to put his fingers to his forehead he saw that his hand was red with Pihay's blood. No one would dare to make the sign of the cross with a blood-stained hand.

Jerome was now wild with rage. He flung his pick and shovel away, took his gun which he had slung from his shoulder by a strap, cocked it, aimed at the hare, and fired. But nothing happened. Then he remembered that he had fired both barrels at Thomas Pihay and had forgotten to reload. In a fury he grabbed the gun by the barrel and raising it against the still motionless animal he dealt with all his strength a blow at it with the butt. The hare contented itself by springing aside, and the wooden stock hit the body with a dull thud. Then the great hare began to run in circles about Jerome and his victim, the circles ever increasing in size.

42

A strange thing then happened. The further away the hare moved the larger did it seem to grow. Unable to endure things any longer Jerome fell in a faint beside Thomas Pihay's body.

4

When Jerome regained consciousness the snow was falling in thick, large flakes. He raised his head and his first look was at Pihay's body which had by now almost disappeared, and a human form was no longer recognisable. But it must be said that Jerome's greatest terror was not the body beside him – it was for the great white hare which, fortunately, had disappeared. He rose to his feet again as though moved by a spring.

He had already given up the idea of burying Pihay, for by now he had neither the courage nor the strength. If he stayed might not the huge hare return? Moreover, most of all, he wanted to get away as quickly as he could. He glanced about him, picked up his gun, pick, and shovel, and with bowed head and bent back he took once more the road to Theux. This time he entered by the door, put everything down, groped his way to his room and buried himself under the bedclothes. A dreadful fever kept him awake for the rest of the night.

In the morning he saw through the panes of the window that the snow was still falling. He got up and went to the window, which looked out onto the garden. Beyond stretched the plain which the snow now covered to the depth of more than a foot. The snow continued falling for another two days until it was at least three feet deep. For all of this time Jerome stayed in his bed. He had no need to invent any excuse for not leaving his room, for although his temperature had dropped it was clear that he was far from well. As he lay in bed he came to the conclusion that his vision of the hare could only be put down to fright.

So he remained with only his crime to face. But for the depth

of snow it would already have been discovered that Thomas
Pihay was dead, but this was still unknown. Jerome hoped that
this providential snow would continue to cover the ground, yet
knew that some day or other it must melt. Meantime, since it
was freezing, the snow remained. He had until a thaw set in,
and until then nobody would find Thomas Pihay's body.

It is true that Jerome thought of flight, but he had no money
and, in any case, the miserable existence he would have to
endure in some foreign land far from his family terrified him
even more than the scaffold. His troubled conscience forced
itself to make excuses for him. In any case, he reasoned that no
one could have seen what had happened and so why should he
rather than anyone else come under suspicion? In all prob-
ability he never would be suspected – he had been seen to go out
on Sunday morning and to return in the evening. But no one
had seen him go out the second time or when he returned.
Again, it was true he had been feverish all night and had been ill
all Monday, but that was no reason for him to have been mixed
up with Pihay's death. Just to be on the safe side, however, he
patched together a story to turn away any suspicions that might
point to him, and waited.

One day when he woke up Jerome saw that the clouds were
low and heavy. When he opened his window a puff of warm air
blew in his face, and soon it started raining. At first it was just a
drizzle but soon the drops became heavier. The thaw had
started, and the moment of truth approached.

In spite of the story he had prepared Jerome's worry increased, his fever returned and he was forced to stay in his bed.
He stayed there all day with the bedclothes tucked up to his
nose. The next day the snow had almost all gone. From his bed
he could see the country and he couldn't take his eyes off it.
Everywhere large patches of black earth thrust through the
snow like islands in the sea.

Suddenly there was a loud noise in the street. At the sound
Jerome broke into one of his sweats. He had no doubt in his

heart that it had to do with Thomas Pihay's death. His first thought was to go and peep through an opening in the curtains, and he even got out of bed to do so but at his first steps his legs failed him. He was dying to ask someone about the noise, which was now increasing and was at that very moment below his window, but he felt certain that his voice would fail him. Then he heard steps on the stairs so he quickly pulled the bedcovers up once again and turned his back to the door.

It was his wife who had come up, but he didn't know that. When she pushed open the door Jerome gave a cry for he thought himself lost.

'Oh, my dear,' she said, 'I am so sorry . . .'

'I was asleep and you woke me up too suddenly.'

'Well, you see, I thought the news would interest you, Jerome.'

'What news?'

'You know that Thomas Pihay disappeared some days ago?'

And Jerome wiped his sweating forehead with the sheet.

'They are bringing his body home,' his wife went on, not taking any notice of Jerome and the movement he had made.

'Ah!' murmured the sick man in a stifled voice. He wished very much, of course, to know what was being said about Pihay's death but he didn't dare to say anything.

His wife went on: 'It seems that he was overcome by the cold and died miserably in the snow.'

'And . . . and . . . his body?' Jerome managed to ask.

'It was eaten by wolves,' answered his wife.

'What? Poor Thomas. But I suppose only the head and limbs?'

'Almost the whole body, for all that was found was the skeleton.'

Jerome breathed again. He thought that if only the skeleton had been recovered any trace of his two shots would have disappeared. His wife continued:

'You see, Jerome, the justice of God is slow, but sooner or

later His hand falls on the guilty and strikes him when he least expects it.'

Jerome groaned. 'Give me a glass of water, I don't feel well. It is the news I have just heard.'

When he brought the glass to his lips his teeth chattered against its rim, and his hand shook so much that half the water spilled on the sheets.

His wife looked at him anxiously. 'Perhaps you are worse than you think, Jerome. Shall I go and get the doctor?'

'No, it's nothing. I have had another attack of fever, but it's the last and I feel I am going to get well.'

Indeed, from that moment thanks to the news he had heard, like a sick person who has overcome a crisis, Jerome got steadily better. By evening, having learned that Thomas Pihay's body had been piously buried under six good feet of earth in the town cemetery, he felt so relieved that he asked his wife to bring the children up to the bedroom, and kissed them as well as their mother, a thing that had not happened since that terrible night. The family's joy was increased when he announced that he felt so well that he was going to get up and come downstairs. His wife offered him her arm, but he refused it. In fact, he descended the stairs without stumbling.

The table had been set for his wife and the two children. 'Well,' Jerome gaily asked, 'aren't I going to have some supper too?'

His wife hastened to lay a fourth place and to bring a chair to the table. Jerome sat down and beat a tattoo on his plate with his knife and fork.

'Goodness, if it's like that,' his wife said, 'there is still in the cellar a bottle of old Burgundy which I put aside for some great occasion. I'll go and get it.'

When she had brought the bottle of wine they all sat down. His wife was so happy that she filled glass after glass for her husband. But suddenly she saw him turn pale and shiver at the same time. Then he ran to his gun which was standing by the fireplace, and did something to it in the darkest corner of the room. He had remembered that the gun had not been reloaded. When he was asked what he had been doing he did not answer.

For more than half an hour after that he paced up and down the room, then he went upstairs and got into his bed without saying another word. During the night his sleep must have been disturbed by some frightful nightmare, because several times he woke up uttering cries of distress and waving his arms about as if to drive away someone or something that was pestering him.

Jerome had seen the great white hare again!

5

The phantom hare would appear at any hour of the day or the night to remind Jerome Palan that his crime had not stayed a secret between him and his maker. That strange apparition constantly dogged his steps and became a torment.

Sometimes Jerome saw the abominable hare beside the fire, warming itself like him, and staring at him with flaming eyes. Sometimes, at meals, the hare would slip under the table and scratch at his legs with its sharp claws. If he wanted to sit at his desk and write he would feel it behind him resting its paws on the back of the chair. During the night the monstrous head of the animal would appear in the alcove, and in vain would Jerome turn over onto his left side, then onto his right. The huge hare was always there facing him. Finally, when the poor man succeeded in falling asleep he was awakened after a few minutes by a tremendous weight on his chest – it was the hare, seated on its haunches, calmly washing its muzzle with its forepaws.

Of course his wife and children saw nothing. As he seemed to be struggling against some sort of imaginary persecution they thought he must be going mad. So there was great sadness in the house.

At last one morning, having suffered from nightmares for too long, Jerome got out of his bed with the calmness of a man who had come to a final decision. He put on his iron-shod boots and buckled above them his big leather gaiters. Then he took down his gun, cleaned both barrels and loaded them with special care, first making sure that the powder was quite dry and putting over it a well-greased felt wad; he next drove this wad firmly home with a ramrod, placed above it a full charge of shot, and finally rammed it all down with the greatest care. All that he had to do now was to prime the gun.

He put the gun over his shoulder, unchained the dogs which bounded joyfully from their kennels, and with them took to the road, the same road which he had tramped when he went to lie in wait in his ambush. His wife accompanied him to the door, happy because she felt that his favourite pastime would distract him from his delusions, and she followed him with her eyes until he had disappeared from view.

This was at the end of January. A heavy mist covered the country and it was thicker in the valleys, but the fields and road were so familiar to Jerome that without any hesitation he went straight to the cross-roads. Soon, ten yards away in a confused shape, he saw the bushes where he had hidden on that fatal night. Suddenly from their far side at the very spot where Thomas Pihay had fallen there sprang up a hare which Jerome instantly recognised by its size as the animal which had so disturbed his peace of mind.

Before Jerome, who must in all honesty have expected its appearance, could put his gun to his shoulder the hare was lost in the mist with Rameau and Spiron coursing after it. Jerome followed them as fast as he was able. A slight breeze had got up and the mist was now clearing away. The dogs were in full cry and the hare was bounding a couple of hundred yards ahead of them, its white coat clearly seen against the red of the heather. Jerome ran with renewed strength.

I can tell you that the hunt was hectic. Hunter, hare and dogs seemed to have muscles of steel. The fields, woods, valleys, hills and streams, all were crossed as though with the help of wings, and this without any of them pausing for a moment for breath. The strange thing, however, was that the huge hare had fled straight ahead like a wily, old wolf. It didn't double back, it didn't follow the streams or ditches, it didn't try to put the dogs on a false scent, and it seemed in no way worried by being hunted. In fact, it went along almost at a quick canter just keeping its distance well ahead of the dogs which had redoubled their speed but in no way shortening the distance separating them from the animal.

Jerome's game-bag got in his way in this mad pursuit so he hurled it away. A branch whipped away his hat and he did not bother to recover it. The hare ran in a vast circle as though it wanted to return to its original starting-point. The hunt had been going on for five hours and now they had reached the bank of the river Ourthe. Jerome, who had had to stop on a small hill to at last get his breath back, never thought that the hare would try to cross it swollen as it was from the melted snow. He reasoned that it would have to turn on its tracks and would at last find itself facing the muzzle of his gun. As for the hare being brought to bay by the dogs, judging by the way in which it had seemed to make sport of them, he had given up all hope of that.

So, counting upon its turning back, Jerome went half way down the hill to the corner of a wood not taking his eyes off the creature; it was sitting on the bank of the river nibbling grass and waiting for the dogs. The dogs came nearer but the hare seemed quite unconcerned, and soon they were only ten yards away. Jerome's heart pounded so much that he could hardly breathe. The distance separating the dogs from the animal was now so small that Ramoneau, which was in the lead, flung himself upon it. But the hare sprang into the torrent to be swept along, and Ramoneau's jaws only snapped the air.

'Oh, wonderful! This time it's going to be drowned,' Jerome shouted.

He raced down to the river-bank at such speed that it was only by the greatest good luck that he didn't fall in. And as he ran he repeated: 'It's going to be drowned! It's going to be drowned!'

The hare, cutting across the current, came ashore unharmed on the opposite bank. The dogs, which like their master had stopped on the brink, flung themselves into the water. But they were not as strong as their quarry and Ramoneau had not the strength to fight against the rush of water, and after a few minutes he was exhausted. He disappeared, then returned to the surface, his paws only feebly beating the surging water. He sank a second time. Jerome descended, or rather rolled down, the bank and threw himself in to help his dog. At that moment Ramoneau's head appeared a third time. Jerome called to him. The poor creature turned its intelligent head towards him and uttered a moan, for at the sound of its master's voice it tried to return to him; it was a fatal thing to do for in attempting to return it was overwhelmed by the current. Ramoneau rolled over several times, once more gave a sad little bark, and made one supreme effort. It turned towards its master and, finally, was swept away downstream.

Jerome had gone in up to his knees. He now plunged right in, swam to his dog, grabbed it, and pulled it back onto the bank. He tried vainly to make it breathe, and to rub its stiff and cold legs. Poor Ramoneau uttered a last groan. It was dead.

At that moment when Jerome in despair was trying to restore his dog to life he heard barking on the other side of the river. Luckier than Ramoneau Spiron had managed to cross and was continuing to hunt the accursed animal. Jerome raised his eyes and saw the great white hare returning on its tracks as though it found an evil pleasure in being present at the death of one of the enemies which had been pursuing it.

Jerome cast a last glance upon his poor and faithful companion, managed to cross the river, and then set out with renewed bitterness in his heart in pursuit of the huge hare. This pursuit lasted until evening, and there is no need for me to tell you that all was in vain. When night began to fall, Spiron, whose barks had for an hour become more and more feeble, lay down and refused to go any further. It was too exhausted to make one more step, so Jerome hoisted the dog on his shoulders. He wondered where he was and, by now, indeed, he was more than twenty-five miles from Theux.

He felt lonelier than he had ever felt before but, strangely, he didn't feel particularly tired and bravely set out on the road for home. Before him stretched, sombre and only broken by a few paths, the forest of Loreé. Without hesitation he entered it. He had been walking for only about ten minutes and had covered at most a couple of hundred yards when he heard behind him the crackle of dried leaves. He turned round. The great hare was following him!

Jerome lengthened his strides, and the hare increased his pace to keep up. Jerome then stopped, put Spiron on the ground, showed him the hare and urged the dog on. But the unfortunate Spiron only contented himself with smelling the scent, uttered a groan, lay down and curled himself up to sleep. Seeing this Jerome decided that the only thing he could do was to use his gun which this time was loaded, well and truly loaded. He cocked both triggers, holding his finger against the tumbler so that the cocking would make no noise. The gun against his shoulder he looked in vain for the phantom hare.

Half maddened with fright and despair Jerome again lifted up Spiron who, still sleeping, was whimpering and no doubt dreaming that he was still hunting the great hare. He then went on his way at a furious pace, without daring to turn again and look behind him.

It was three in the morning before he reached home. Needless to say, his wife was very worried and was awaiting his return intending to tell him how thoughtless he had been. But when she saw how distressed he was she said nothing. Then, as he let Spiron slip from his shoulders, she took his gun from him.

You will remember that he had lost both his game-bag and his hat. She made him go to bed at once, and then took him a big bowl of hot spiced wine and sat on the edge of his bed. She took him by both of his hands and without saying anything began to weep quietly.

Jerome was very touched and after a few minutes thought he felt that by sharing his secret with her he could unload half of his troubles. He was quite sure that she would say nothing to anyone, and so he confessed everything. She did not reproach him. She did not burst out with any harsh words about his fatal passion for hunting, the cause of so much misfortune. Quite the contrary – she made excuses for the violence that had resulted in Thomas Pihay's death. Without condemning the dead she recalled the just complaints which Jerome had against him. Finally, she took her husband in her arms and consoled him as a mother does a well-loved child, and tried to give him a little peace of mind.

Then she said: 'Look, Jerome, you must recognise in all this the hand of God. It was He who brought the unfortunate Thomas in front of the muzzle of your gun to punish him for his wickedness to you. But it is also God who, to make you see your disbelief in Him, allows this malign and phantom creature to torment you.'

Jerome sighed, but he did not scoff at his wife as he certainly would once have done.

She went on: 'You must go to our curé and tell him everything. He will help you to drive away the demon which is in the wicked hare.'

But Jerome protested at this suggestion. 'Oh, yes,' he said, 'go to the curé so that he can denounce me to the prince-bishop. What an idea! I've had enough dealings with him and will take good care not to fall into his hands again. You are mad, wife, to suggest such a thing. In all that has happened there has been neither the hand of God nor the devil.'

'Then what is it?' his wife exclaimed in despair.

'It has all been pure chance and my imagination. I must kill this wretched hare. When I have seen it dead at my feet, quite dead, my mind will of its own accord become calm and I shall no longer remember what has happened.'

His poor wife resigned herself. She knew only too well how useless it would be to argue with him.

6

After resting for two days, a rest greatly needed by both himself and the dog, and the dog even more than the master, Jerome set out again. As before he put up the hare at the same place, which was all the more strange because more than thirty people passed by there every day. And, as before, the hare baffled all pursuit with Jerome returning home sad and depressed with his new game-bag empty.

Every two or three days for a whole month Jerome continued his bitter struggle with always the same result, and at the end of the month poor Spiron died of exhaustion. His own strength flagging and Spiron dead Jerome was forced to give up this fantastic hunting. While it had gone on he had done no work and now his family was poverty-stricken.

At first his wife had somehow managed by economies and, afterwards, by selling sometimes a piece of jewellery and sometimes bit by bit the furniture. Soon the house was almost empty and the walls bare. There no longer remained a single thing having any value whatever, and on the day that Spiron had died she had to confess to Jerome that there was no bread in the house.

Jerome took from his pocket a gold watch that had been a family possession for many, many years and which he treasured so much that his wife had not dared to ask him to sell it. Well, Jerome handed it to her without saying a word. His wife went to Liége where she sold it for nine louis. On her return she gave Jerome the money. He looked at it covetously, and yet somehow with hesitation. Finally he took four of the coins and asked: 'For how long do you think we can live on five louis?'

His wife thought quickly. 'With economy for two months,' she replied.

'Two months?' Jerome repeated, 'that's far more than I need. Before two months have passed I will have had that big hare jugged, or I will be dead.'

His wife started crying.

'Don't worry,' Jerome continued, 'with these four louis I am going to Luxembourg. I know a poacher there who still has some of the breed of poor Flambeau and Ramette. If he has two dogs for sale may the devil take me if within a fortnight I don't make you a muff out of the skin of that accursed hare.'

So Jerome left one morning for Luxembourg. He found his poacher and bought from him a dog and a bitch, Rocador and Tambelle. He returned home in triumph.

Next day, at dawn, he was in the fields. But the great hare was more cunning and stronger than any dog no matter what its breed. It out-distanced the descendants of Flambeau and Ramette as it had done Rameau and Spiron. Jerome, however, had become wiser through experience. He did not hunt the hare for more than three or four hours at a time, and at last he decided that strength was useless against it and so he restored to trickery.

He carefully stopped up the holes in the hedges which the hare was accustomed to use, leaving only one or two open and in these with the greatest care he put nooses. Then he lay in wait nearby, as much to help the dogs if they should be caught as to have the chance of shooting the hare. But the wily animal laughed at all this. It scented and understood what had been done, and made new holes in the hedges close to those which had been blocked. From whichever direction the breeze came it scented Jerome and was well outside the range of his gun. It was enough to drive anyone out of his mind.

The two months passed and the children had still not enjoyed their jugged hare, their mother still had no muff. Jerome was still alive, if such an existence could be called living. He had no rest, either night or day. He had become as yellow as an old citron-melon. His skin was like parchment and seemed to cling to his bones. But an almost superhuman strength sustained him, and the terrible hunts that he endured almost every day now showed the strength that was still left in him.

Two more months passed. The family had to live on credit, and then by borrowing. At last one morning the unfortunate family were thrown out of their house by the bailiffs.

'Oh!' Jerome lamented, 'all of this would be nothing if only I could lay my hands on that wretched hare.'

He was able to find an empty hut at the other end of the town. He slung his gun over his shoulder as though he was leaving to hunt, took each child by the hand, whistled to his dogs, signed to his wife to follow him, and left his old home without even a backward glance. It seemed to his wife that life was deserting her when they left the house where she had been happy for so long.

When they arrived at the miserable lodging her first thought was to pray. So joining her hands and kneeling before her husband she begged him to recognise the hand of God, and asked the Almighty to exorcise the demon which seemed to have possessed him. Jerome, embittered by misfortune, took no notice and pointing to his gun merely replied: 'Just let this scoundrelly hare pass me forty yards away. Then I will have absolution.'

But more than ten times after he had said this Jerome fired at the hare from forty yards, from thirty, even from twenty, and more than ten times did he miss it. In this way autumn was reached, and very soon it would be the anniversary of the night that had wrecked Jerome's whole life.

On the evening before Saint Hubert's day Jerome was thinking over some fresh idea. It might have been seven o'clock. He was sitting beside a miserable peat fire and opposite him was his wife with the children on her knees trying to keep warm. Suddenly the door opened and the landlord of an inn came into the room.

'Monsieur Palan,' he said, 'would you like to earn a good day's wages tomorrow?'

Good wages were so rare that Jerome no longer believed in such a windfall. He replied by shaking his head.

'You refuse?'

'I am not refusing, but what I want to know is how I am going to earn a good day's wages.'

'It is quite easy. I have two visitors who have come to Theux to hunt. Will you show them the country where the best game is tomorrow?'

Jerome, who no doubt had intended spending the next day in pursuit of the great hare, was about to say he had other things to do, but his wife guessing what he was thinking pointed at the two hungry children and he kept silent.

'Very well,' he said at last, with a sigh.

'Good. Come for them at half-past eight. I have no need to tell you to be punctual for I can remember that when you were an apothecary you were only too much so if you had to open a boil on me.'

'At half-past eight then,' Jerome agreed.

The innkeeper went out, led by Jerome's wife who was thanking him profusely.

Jerome started his preparations for the next day. He filled his powder-horn and his bullet-pouch, then he cleaned his gun and put it on the table. For her part his wife watched very thoughtfully while all this was going on as if she was thinking up some plan. At last they went to bed.

Jerome slept soundly and awoke later than he usually did. When he opened his eyes he was in bed alone. He called out to his wife and children, but no one answered and he thought that they could only be in the patch of a garden. He got out of bed and dressed quickly as the cuckoo-clock struck eight and he was afraid of missing his appointment. When he was fully dressed he started looking for his gun, powder-horn, bullet-pouch and game-bag. They had gone, and yet he clearly remembered putting them all on the table. He rummaged about in all the corners and turned everything over, but search as he might he could find nothing.

He rushed outside calling for his wife to come and help him, but neither she nor the children were anywhere to be seen. He then saw that the kennels of Rocador and Tambelle were empty. At that moment the clock struck half-past eight and he hadn't a moment to lose. Not wishing to lose the windfall promised him he ran to the inn to borrow from the landlord what he needed. There, finding the hunters ready to leave, he told them of his misadventure and they lent him a gun and game-bag.

The three of them were about to set out when Jerome saw his wife hurrying towards them. She was carrying everything he could not find and the dogs were running at her side.

'Wait!' she called out, 'you are going without your gun and the dogs.'

'Where on earth were they? I couldn't find them anywhere.'

'Of course you couldn't. I had locked up the gun and the other things so that the children couldn't play with them. I took the dogs to the butcher's for some scraps he had promised.'

'What's happened to the children?'

'They came with me . . . But look, these gentlemen are getting impatient. I won't wish you good luck because they say that that brings bad luck. But something tells me that you will come back happier than when you left.'

Jerome looked doubtful. He knew only too well that things don't always turn out as well as they might be expected to.

He was so used to heading towards the cross-roads that from sheer force of habit he led the hunters there. The dogs were unleashed and set to work. For the first time they seemed to have difficulty in picking up any scent. But they became keener when they came close to a path and Jerome, used to the habit of his great hare suddenly and boldly appearing in front of the dogs, supposed that it had not passed the night here and that Rocador and Tambelle had picked up the scent of some other hare.

But just then one of the hunters stooped to look at a spoor as they were crossing the damp path and exclaimed: 'Come and look at this! Here is a hare's fresh footprint. Have you ever seen such a big hare, Monsieur Palan?'

A single glance was enough for him to recognise to whom the enormous footprint belonged. Yes, certainly, Monsieur Palan had seen such a hare, for it was his very one, his nightmare, his terror. His face darkened as he thought that if bad luck willed that the two strangers had as bad sport as he had become used to he could not expect the good wages on which he was depending. Meantime the barking of the dogs grew more lively for they were getting closer to the hare, and so the two hunters separated to wait for the hare to pass between them.

Jerome led one of them back to the cross-roads because he was curious to see someone else fire at the creature, and hoped that half an ounce of lead fired by a complete stranger might break the spell. He was at long last realising that, all along, he had been dealing with a creature possessed, if not with magical powers, then something very close to them. Yet, even as he recognised the footprint as that of the great hare he had hunted for a year he still could not understand its behaviour, for it travelled straight like a wolf whereas a hare after a wide circuit returned to its form like a rabbit.

And now the curious thing was that the dogs, which during the last few days had shown little interest in hunting as if they knew beforehand that everything was useless, seemed filled with an incomprehensible energy and strength. Their barking was furious as they followed the animal on its trail. Poor Jerome could neither believe his eyes nor his ears. It seemed to him impossible that this was his old enemy, but at last at one of the paths leading back to the cross-roads he saw it. Most decidedly it was the one. It was of tremendous size and had its white hair. It was heading straight towards them, and Jerome touched the elbow of the hunter and pointed to the animal.

'Yes, I see it,' he said.

The great white hare still came towards them.

'At thirty yards and between the shoulders,' Jerome whispered to his companion.

'Of course,' and he slowly raised his gun. The hare stopped, sat down, and pretended to listen. Jerome's heart beat wildly. The hunter fired, and as the wind was blowing away from the hare a few seconds passed before the effects of the shot could be seen.

'Good heavens!' Jerome exclaimed.

'What? Have I missed it?'

'I think so. Look, do you see it?' And he pointed to the hare which was now slowly climbing a slope. The hunter fired his second barrel, and this was as useless as the first. Jerome remained stock-still. He seemed to have forgotten that he, too, had a gun ready to fire.

'Fire at it! Fire at it!' shouted his companion.

Jerome took aim.

'Ah!' said the other, 'it's too far away now.'

He had no sooner spoken than Jerome fired. Although the hare was, in fact, about a hundred yards away he hit it and it rolled over several times, and then stayed stretched on the ground.

One of the hunters ran and grabbed it by the hind legs and Jerome, out of breath, mad with joy, and unable to believe his eyes, finished it off with a blow on the back of its neck. It was a blow which could have felled an ox.

The visitors were amazed at the size of the brute, and were delighted with the way the day's hunting had started. Jerome didn't say a word, but I can tell you that he was even more delighted than his companions. It seemed to him that a mountain had been lifted from his chest. He breathed freely, and the earth, the trees, and the sky were all rose-coloured.

He took the big hare from the hunter who was holding it and thrust it into his game-bag. Although it was very heavy it seemed to weigh nothing to him, and every now and then he pulled the bag round to make sure that it hadn't disappeared. There it was, glassy-eyed, doubled up on itself, only its legs sticking out and so long were they that they reached to Jerome's shoulders. The dogs, too, seemed happy and showed their delight by leaping and barking. They reached up on their hind paws to smell the game-bag and to lick the blood dripping from it.

The rest of the day continued to be as good as it had started. Jerome showed himself to be a reliable guide and led his new friends to wherever game could be found, better than any hound or spaniel could have done. Although the season was already well advanced they were able to shoot five brace of wood-grouse as well as a good deal else. So pleased were the two hunters that they gave Jerome a gold louis and invited him to have supper at the inn with them that night.

At any other time Jerome would have refused because his mind would have been so taken up with the vision of the phantom white hare, but its death had completely changed things and he thought he might just as well round off the day's work with a celebration. However, he arranged things so that he returned to Theux by a different way from his companions, for he had made two decisions – first, to give the gold louis to his wife so that there could be a celebration in his poor dwelling, as well as at the inn. Then he also wished to show his loved ones that abominable big hare which was now so harmless.

His wife was waiting for him for all the world as though she was expecting good news. As soon as she saw him approaching she hastened to meet him.

'Well?' she asked.

Jerome opened his game-bag and pulled from it the great hare to show it to her, and shaking it by the paws, 'Well,' he answered, 'you can see.'

'The phantom white hare!' she said joyously.

'Yes. It will no longer come and scratch my legs when I am sitting at the table. And *I* killed it with a fine shot. The lead must have been driven by a devil of a wind to carry so far.'

'No, Jerome, no, by the wind of the good God.'

'What can you mean?'

'Listen, Jerome, and be grateful. This morning without saying a word to you I went to mass and prayed to Saint Hubert to bless your gun and dogs. It was he who exorcised the curse and performed a miracle with your shot. Have you still any doubts?'

Jerome hadn't the courage to reply; he gave her only a half-mocking smile.

'Jerome! Jerome!' his wife went on, 'I hope that after this miracle you will no longer have any doubts in God.'

'I have no more doubts.'

'Very well then. Grant me just one favour. If you do it will make me very happy.'

'What is that?'

'You will be passing the church on your way, Jerome. Go in and pray, and give your thanks.'

'But I don't remember any prayers,' Jerome answered. 'What should I do in church not knowing any prayers?'

'You simply say "Thank you, God" and make the sign of the cross.'

'Tomorrow,' Jerome said, 'perhaps tomorrow.'

'But, unhappy man,' his wife cried out in despair, 'anything can happen between today and tomorrow. Jerome, in the name of your wife and children, go into the church. Repeat what I have told you and make the sign of the cross.'

His wife took him by the arm to lead him towards the church.

'Not now,' Jerome said impatiently, 'these gentlemen are waiting for me at the inn, and I don't want their supper to get cold. Here is the money they gave me. Buy what you like, and be easy, for I promise to go to mass tomorrow and on Sunday too, and to confession at Easter. There, does that make you happy?'

The poor woman gave a deep sigh and let her husband's arm fall. She stayed motionless where she stood and followed him with her eyes as he walked away. Then she went home and instead of preparing supper she prayed.

Meantime all was going well at the inn. Bottles followed one after the other and Jerome had the pleasure of renewing acquaintance with some of the wines he was used to drinking in the days when he was prosperous. Time passed quickly, so quickly that the clock struck twelve when everyone thought that it could only be about ten o'clock.

The chimes were still echoing when, suddenly, a strong wind made the flames of the lamps flicker. The visitors as well as Jerome felt a chill go through their bones, and with one movement they all rose to their feet. Just then they seemed to hear something resembling a moan from the corner of the room where they had put their guns and game.

'What was that?' one of the hunters asked.

'I don't know', the other replied. 'What did *you* hear?'

'Something like somebody in pain.'

'Let's go and look.'

They made a movement to go to the corner, looking to see if Jerome would go with them. But he was standing, pale, shaking like a leaf, and speechless. He was staring at his own game-bag which was making strange movements in the shadows. One of his shaking hands seized that of one of his companions, while the other covered his eyes.

The great white hare had pushed its muzzle through the opening of the game-bag, between the two buttons that held it closed. Then, after the muzzle, the head appeared, and after the head the body. And as if it were upon the heather in some piece of waste land it began to browse peacefully upon the green tops of a nearby heap of carrots. While it browsed it gave Jerome one of those terrible and flashing glances which had almost driven him mad. He gave a cry as if his heart had been pierced, and without saying a word, sprang to the door, opened it, and fled across the fields.

The hare left its carrot tops and raced after him.

Jerome's wife, waiting at the door and hoping for his return, saw him pass without even noticing her, without answering her call. Behind him bounded the great hare, bigger still than it had ever been. It could have been said that there were two phantoms, so rapidly did they pass.

On the following morning Jerome's body was found on the very spot where, a year before, that of Thomas Pihay, had been discovered. He seemed to have been dead for some hours. He was lying on his back, his hands holding the big hare by the neck, and his fingers held it so tightly that it was impossible to remove the abominable animal. Needless to say, it, too, was quite dead.

The money which Jerome had received from the two hunters paid for his coffin, a mass, and his burial.

PETER AND HIS GOOSE

Peter's father and mother had died when he was quite young. They had worked hard and had lived modestly, and the farm that now belonged to Peter was well-stocked with cows, not to mention fowls, ducks and geese. There were also barns filled with grain and haystacks as high as mountains. Peter was very pleased with his new freedom to do whatever he wished, and spent most of his time idly strolling about the fields, or fishing, whenever he felt like it.

But Farmer Peter, for that was how he liked to be called after the death of his parents, had forgotten that the grain and the hay would not last forever. He never worried about tomorrow, and what gave him most pleasure was to lie in his bed from eight at night until eight next morning, and then on the grass from eight in the morning till eight at night.

Of course he had to eat, and he did so four times a day – at ten in the morning, at midday, and at three and five o'clock in the afternoon. You can see that there was not a great deal to be said in praise of Peter, but you will see what happened as a result of his laziness.

One day when, as he always did, he was lying in the sun and thinking of nothing an old goose waddled up to him, saluted him by bending her long neck, and spoke to him in a quiet, clear voice:

'Farmer Peter, how do you do?'

Peter turned over and opened his eyes wide for, to be quite truthful, I should tell you that he was most surprised to hear a goose speak to him. But he wasn't scared and answered: 'Many thanks for asking, Mrs Goose, I am very well.'

Then he closed his eyes again without being polite enough to ask the goose how she was keeping. But the goose, after a moment's silence and seeing that he was starting to snore, called out:

'Wake up, Farmer Peter, I have wanted to talk to you for a long time, and I should tell you that it is something you would like to hear.'

'Oh,' Peter replied, 'I want to sleep, and I am sure that what you have to say will take too long.'

'Very well. So you think I am only a goose?'

'Of course I know you are a goose. Why are you waking me from a lovely sleep when I know that you can have nothing very interesting to say?'

'Now listen carefully Farmer Peter. I am not only a goose, I am a fairy as well.'

'Really!' Peter said, for his mother when she was rocking him to sleep when he was a very small boy had told him about fairies.

'Yes, indeed I am a fairy,' the goose went on, 'and each egg that I lay gives the lucky owner the chance to wish for whatever he wants when he breaks the shell. There are no more than fifteen eggs for each person, and as it happens I have fifteen eggs in my nest now. So, you lucky boy, you can have all of them and wish for whatever you want.'

The goose had barely finished speaking than Peter forgot all about wanting to sleep. He got up, searched for the nest, and when he had found it counted the eggs there. There were, indeed, exactly fifteen.

'Well,' asked the goose, who had waddled after him, 'haven't I told you the truth?'

'Up and until now, yes,' Peter answered. 'It is quite true you have laid fifteen eggs, but I wonder if the rest of what you have told me is also true.'

'Try them,' was all the goose said.

Peter quickly took an egg from the nest and was just about to throw it on the ground . . .

'Just a moment, Farmer Peter, you must first make a wish or else the breaking of the shell will spoil everything.'

'Good, then what will I wish for,' Peter wondered.

'Follow my advice,' said the goose, 'wish to be a bird, for I can tell you that it is lovely to be one.'

'Oh my word, yes, I have so often watched the swallows and the cranes high above the clouds and wanted to be a bird. So, I wish, I wish to be a bird!' And he threw the egg against a stone and broke the shell.

At once his boots flew off and, like his hat which hung in the air for a moment, disappeared into the distance. In all the commotion he fell flat on his back. But as soon as he got to his feet again he went to a stream to look at his reflection, and saw that he had become an enormous crane. Now, Peter did not feel at all comfortable in his new feathers; he did not dare to try and walk far on his long legs with his big beak going clackety-clack. And as he clacked he gave, as well as he was able, little cries of fright.

'Oh what shall I do?' he cried, for he was still able to speak, 'I don't like this and I don't want to be a bird anymore. I want to be as I was before.'

In about a minute he was Peter once again. He looked about him. He saw his boots far away, and his hat further away still, and rushed to put them all on again. Then he waved his arms about like a windmill to make sure that they were not wings and that he was really himself.

'Oof,' he said, 'that was a nasty trick to play on me.'

'You are wrong,' replied the goose, 'it wasn't a trick at all. You see, you were so quick to find out if a wish could be granted that you didn't take time to think what sort of a bird you wanted to be. The genie had just heard you mention a crane, and it believed that that was the one bird above all you would like to become – so there you were, a crane.'

'Not only did I not want to be a crane,' Peter said, 'but I really, honestly, didn't want to be any sort of bird. No, I want to be something important, like a soldier. Yes, a soldier, an officer, just like one of those who passed through the village a week ago.'

And taking another egg he did what he had been told to be before. The egg smashed, and as it did it made the noise of a whole battery of cannon being fired.

Peter was, indeed, dressed as an officer. He seemed to be in the middle of some great battle, or taking part with an army in besieging a town. Bullets whistled round his ears, shells hit the ground near him to explode not far away. Although he was wearing an officer's uniform he hadn't a soldier's courage.

'This is dreadful,' he shouted, 'and I want to be away from it all.'

At the very moment he spoke a bullet hit the top of his helmet and knocked him over so that he fell on his back. Peter thought he had been killed and lay where he was, then, not hearing any more noise he lifted his head and looked around. He was lying on a heap of straw in the farmyard, and the old goose who was honking away close by looked at him in surprise.

Peter sat up. He wiped the sweat from his forehead and licked gunpowder from his lips. More than anything else he was very frightened. Then he noticed that the apple-tree in his neighbour's garden was covered with lovely ripe fruit.

'Ah! I'm so thirsty,' he said to himself, 'how I would like suddenly to see my hat filled to its brim with some of those apples.'

And this time, without saying anything to the goose, he grabbed an egg and broke its shell. Just as he did that he found himself on the highest branch of the tree with his hat full of apples. But poor Peter had no time to enjoy the fruit that he had asked for, for the angry owner of the orchard appeared armed with a long stick and whacked the thief's shoulders.

Peter very quickly wished to be back where he had come from, and landed home again with a thump.

'Why didn't you climb down and save yourself from a beating?' the goose asked.

But instead of answering that question Peter said: 'Look, I must talk to you.' And the pair of them went into the farmhouse and sat down together to discuss the best thing to do.

All of a sudden Peter said: 'I've got a fine idea!'

'And what is it?' the old goose asked.

'I'm going to get an egg and then wish for lots of money. Upon my word that will solve everything.'

He went for an egg, came back, and had hardly broken it than the lid of the bread-bin lifted, being pushed up by all the money that had filled the bin to overflowing. Peter rushed to it, tied the lid to the wall, and gazed in rapture at the treasure. For her part the goose flopped onto a chair and, stretching her neck, stared at all the money too. The two of them stayed where they were wrapped in their thoughts until the evening.

Then, when night fell, Peter hunted about for the biggest padlocks he could find and put them on the door in case of thieves. He had never locked the door before. He found he couldn't go to sleep and towards midnight got out of bed to see the goose plodding backwards and forwards in front of the bread-bin, just like a watchman in front of a bank. At last, at about two in the morning finding that sleep would not come to him, Peter went to the window to count the stars until dawn came.

Although Peter, as it is easy to see, was a boy with not much imagination or ambition, he was now beginning to understand that it had been very silly of him to wish to be a crane, an officer, and then to have a hunger for apples. Indeed, this last wish was the silliest of them all. But now he understood that his new fortune could be the cause of a lot of worry. So, when the goose came to the window, he said:

'I must tell you, Mrs Goose, that I think my three first wishes

were stupid. But now, with all my money, is there any safe way
of keeping it so that only when I need a pocketful of gold or
silver I can come and get it?'

The goose gave Peter a mocking look.

'Well, why not be a king? Kings have no worries of that kind.
They have men who look after his treasure and give him money
when he wants it. He has soldiers, too, guarding the treasury.'

'I never knew that,' Peter replied. 'Then I will be a king, and
this very moment.'

So he took one of the eggs which, in some miraculous way,
were always near him and threw it on the doorstep.

In the twinkling of an eye Peter found himself seated on a
throne in the middle of a magnificent room. He was wearing a
starched strawberry-coloured ruff, a long wig, and he had
a heavy crown on his head. All around him people were bowing
low and greeting him. He did not know how to reply to their
greetings so, instead, he demanded when breakfast would be
served. His majesty was told that it would not be until nine
o'clock.

Now, Peter was very hungry indeed. I have already told you
that he always woke up at eight – and at the same time as he
opened his eyes he opened his mouth. So he asked if, while he
was waiting for his breakfast, he could have a cup of coffee and,
perhaps, a little cheese to go on with. But he was told that as for
the coffee he must have forgotten that he had already had a
cup, and as for the cheese, why, that was something that a man
who was king could never eat.

Just then Peter saw the goose bowing to him. She asked him
with a cackle of laughter: 'Is your majesty finding everything as
he wishes?'

'Pouah!' Peter said. 'If being a king means that he cannot
have what he wants, not even a piece of cheese to nibble when
he's hungry, and when he does have breakfast served he has to
eat it wearing a stiff ruff which chokes him and makes it
difficult to use a knife and fork, I can tell you this, Mrs Goose,

that I would much rather not be one. As there is a warm sun shining I am going into the palace garden and stretch out on the grass.'

He had just finished speaking to the goose when a startled footman came and said: 'But you cannot do that, your majesty, you might risk your precious life.'

'And why,' Peter demanded, 'should I risk my precious life as you call it by lying on the grass?'

'Because I have just been told of a most frightful plot against your majesty.'

'You?'

'Yes, me.'

'Then are you my chief of police?'

'Your majesty may laugh, but Mrs Goose has given me that job.'

'The deuce,' said Peter, 'and who wants to kill me?'

'Thirty men are coming during the day and have sworn the most terrible oaths that if you do not die from a bullet you will not escape the sword. But if you *do* by good luck escape the sword then you will most certainly not escape being poisoned.'

'So, Mrs Goose,' Peter said, turning away from the footman, 'what have you to say about all this?'

'I say,' the goose replied, 'that it is all most serious unless, of course, the chief of police is telling you an untruth.'

'But why should he think up such a story?'

'That's easy to answer. I have known chiefs of police who have only kept their jobs by thinking up a new plot each week. It may sound simple, but some by this means have held onto their jobs for eight, or even ten, years.'

'Oh! Oh!' Peter exclaimed, 'please get out of my way, my friend.'

'Why?'

'To let me pass.'

'And where are you going?'

'Most of all I want something to eat, even a piece of ham, and then to lie on the grass in the sun. There is a smoked ham hanging in my kitchen, and that lovely lawn near the door of my farmhouse. I am going home.'

'Just a moment, your majesty,' the goose said, 'When I came over to you at the window early this morning I brought the rest of my eggs with me just in case you wanted to make another wish. That will make it easier for you. After all, just to go home to get a slice of ham to eat seems to me to be rather a silly idea.'

'Upon my word,' Peter answered, 'I know what I want, exactly what I want, and I have a better idea. Where are the eggs?'

'The basket is under that chair, your majesty.'

The clothes Peter was wearing were so stiff that he could only bend down with great difficulty, but he did manage to get hold of an egg.

As he did so he said to himself: 'After all, no one is going to tell an admiral of the fleet when he can eat and what he can do, and sailing the seas he has a splendid life with more freedom than most people. Besides, if I remember right, an admiral's uniform is very grand.'

It must be said that Peter, once he had made up his mind, wasted no time and he quickly broke the egg. At once he was changed into an admiral, an admiral who was all of seventy years old with a patch over one eye as well as a wooden leg. And he had a mahogany crutch to help him stomp about the deck.

'Oh, good heavens!' Peter shouted. 'I wanted to be an admiral, but not an old broken-down one with only one eye and a wooden leg who is likely to die at any moment!'

'But,' the goose answered, 'allow me to tell you that it is most unusual for an admiral to be not twenty years old yet. And in any case not many reach those heights by doing nothing else than just lazing about at home.'

Peter groaned. 'How silly can you be, Mrs Goose, and as I am afraid of some calamity happening to me in this stupid uniform I want to be my old self again.'

71

The wish being made Peter found himself in the farmhouse kitchen again with his goose perched on a table facing him.

There was one thing that the goose hadn't noticed, and that was the rage that Peter was in with his flushed face. On the table was a knife. He snatched it up and rushed towards the bird which he thought had tempted him into so many disagreeable adventures. But the goose was not going to be killed so easily. As she flapped away she called out in a very loud voice that he was most ungrateful, and told him of the wonderful chances he had been offered and which he had missed. She went on to say that *he* was the silly goose and that she was the one who was sensible. She ended her speech by slapping his face hard with her wings.

'Listen to me, my friend,' she went on after a pause, 'I have sometimes seen you looking through books of travel and adventure. Wouldn't you like to visit foreign lands?'

'As a matter of fact,' Peter replied when he had calmed down, 'those kinds of books do interest me very much and the two I like best are "Robinson Crusoe" and "Gulliver's Travels".'

'Alright then, why don't you become another Robinson Crusoe?'

'Why, that's not a bad idea. If I were a Robinson Crusoe I would have an island all to myself. I wish to be one! I wish to be one!' he shouted, and took an egg and cracked it with his foot.

Unluckily for him Peter had forgotten to mention the size of his island and he found himself sitting on a not very large rock. Indeed, like Robinson Crusoe, Peter was on a deserted island – and what an island! The rock was six feet long and about as wide, giving him just enough room to keep fairly dry. The wind blew, the sea roared about him, and seagulls flew near giving their sad calls. But for how long could he stay dry as the waves hurled themselves against the rock, breaking on it as if they wanted to wash it away.

'Oh, how unhappy I am,' Peter wailed, shivering with cold

and fright. 'How I would like to return to my own warm house. But I would only be able to do that if I had a fishtail and fins, and I am so scared of the sea that even if I were a fish I don't think I would dare venture into it.'

He had hardly finished speaking when he heard a noise behind him which he could not recognise. He turned his head to see where it came from and saw Mrs Goose balancing herself on the top of a wave and squawking and flapping her wings.

'Peter,' she managed to call out, 'don't you know that there are different kinds of fish?'

'Yes, of course you are right. I had forgotten. There are flying-fish. Where are the eggs?'

'On your right, in a hollow in the rock.'

'I suppose you know there are not many left, Mrs Goose.'

The goose seemed to take no notice of what Peter had just said. But after a while she asked: 'Do you want to stay on the island?'

'My goodness no! I want to leave here as quickly as possible.'

So Peter broke an egg and wished to become a flying-fish. At once he felt his ears stretch to become long transparent fins, whilst his legs joined together and became slender; as for his feet they turned into a magnificent shiny tail. At the same time he felt that he must dive into the sea.

For a few minutes Peter, who you will remember was very frightened of the sea, swam happily about and began to enjoy being a fish. But then when he went deeper he met a monstrous fish more than fifty times bigger than he was, and with a big mouth wide open ready to swallow him.

At once poor Peter turned and swam as fast as he could to the surface, and using his fins as wings skimmed along the water. He enjoyed doing this, wetting his wings every now and then on the top of a wave, when he heard a piercing cry from the clouds which made him tremble. He turned on one side and saw a white spot in the sky which grew bigger and bigger the faster it flew down to him. It was an albatross, and these birds are very fond of the taste of flying-fish. Its beak was open, its talons spread out, and unlucky Peter felt himself already half-eaten.

He was so terrified that his fins seemed to lose their strength and folded limply to his sides, so that he dived into the sea so fast that he was nearly five feet beneath the surface as the bird's beak skimmed along the water. But he had just regained the use of his fins when the giant fish from which he had already escaped, and which was not going to let him get away again, came from behind to within a foot or two of his tail.

'I'm not going to stay a minute longer in the sea or the air being a wretched flying-fish,' Peter murmured. 'I want to go quickly to dry land and to be anywhere near my farmhouse.'

The wish was no sooner made than Peter found himself lying worn out with tiredness on the road that passed near his farm. He got up and went to the farmhouse and kicked the door open. In the kitchen was the old goose, who nearly fell over in fright. She had every reason to feel frightened for Peter's change back to himself was not quite complete. He still had the head of a fish, which made him look very queer; but slowly his own head came back again, and I must tell you here that as the eggs became fewer and fewer their power to make rapid changes grew weaker.

This last adventure had almost cured Peter of his craze for breaking the goose's eggs. He spent the next seven or eight days quietly enough either lying beside the fire or, if it was warm enough, on the grass, for he was quite tired out by all the changes he had gone through.

From time to time, however, some fresh idea flitted through his mind, but he never even touched the eggs that were left. And now he didn't sleep as much as he used to. He strolled about his farm with the old goose waddling at his heels telling him, as all old geese do, the gossip of the farmyard.

In the end all this dawdling and gossip so wearied Peter that he decided he must break another egg. But what could he wish to be? Certainly not a big ungainly bird, nor a soldier risking death at any moment, nor money which he would have to guard with his life, nor a king unable to eat when he wanted to and tortured in his stiff silk ruff like the old knights in their armour, nor an admiral blind in one eye and lame, too, having to walk with the help of a crutch, nor living on a rock which called itself an island and being lashed by gales, nor, and this most certainly not, a flying-fish being chased by a shark and an albatross.

Oh no, Peter wanted an easy life in which he could sleep and eat whenever he wished to and for as long as he liked, with nothing else to do. It was all very difficult.

While Peter was deep in thought he heard near him a cheerful grunt, and so he tiptoed to the pigsty. Under the roof and beside a wall he saw what seemed to be such a picture of idleness and happiness as could not be found anywhere else in the world. There lay on its fresh straw a very large and very fat pig, its eyes half-closed and only moving its ears and curly tail when it was bothered by flies.

'Goodness me!' he exclaimed. 'Why hadn't I thought before of being a pig? As sure as my name's Peter that would be a lovely life. A pig has plenty to eat and no worry as to where it comes from. It can sleep as much as it wants to, and it can chase flies away with its ears and tail without even waking up. What a wonderful life!'

We know now that Peter had only to stretch out a hand to pick up an egg, and he took one more and broke the shell. He soon found himself lying on some clean straw with a feeding-trough of his own within reach of his snout.

It is fair to say that his first feeling was one of pure content-ment. It was marvellous to stretch his short legs in the lovely warmth of the sun that came through the opening in the roof of his sty, and he ate greedily some excellent apples that had been put in his trough. Then he fell asleep, just like his companion next door. He didn't seem to have been sleeping long before the sun starting going down when a rough-looking man came without knocking into Peter's shed, and felt him all over to see how nice and fat he was.

This was all the more disagreeable to Peter, for when he was the Peter as we first knew him he was ticklish. If he could have spoken he would have told the man how much he disliked what was being done to him, and would have asked him to let him lie in peace. But the man was not interested in what was disagreeable to Peter and went on feeling and prodding him in his most tender parts, and seemed very pleased. Then, humming a little tune, the man started to roll up his sleeves as if he was going to do some work. As it was clear that this work had something to do with Peter the pig he opened fully one eye so that he wouldn't be taken by surprise.

The man, however, didn't seem to be uneasy when he noticed this, and to the unutterable terror of our hero, he took from his belt the most frightful looking knife. Then, with the knife between his teeth, he grabbed Peter by an ear and a foot and held him with his knees. Feeling Peter's neck for the right place, and having found it, he put his thumb on it and took the knife from between his teeth with his other hand.

Peter knew only too well that if he waited a moment longer he would suffer a terrible death.

'Good heavens!' he managed to call out in a voice so unlike anything that could be expected to come from a pig's snout, 'I am not a pig, you dreadful man!'

The butcher very quickly dropped his knife, and his legs shook so much that he could no longer grip Peter. He jumped backwards, and when he was out of the shed he fled as fast as his legs could carry him.

As Peter's arms and legs had become once again those of a human being, although his head remained that of a pig as the magic was no longer working as fast as it once did, he seized the knife and started to run after his persecutor determined to make *him* feel the sharpness of the blade. The man looked back and seeing that he was being chased by a monster with a human

body and a pig's head shouted with fear and ran towards a
stream to throw himself in. By now Peter had his own head
again. He dropped the knife and holding his sides could not
help roaring with laughter.

Peter went back to his farmhouse still laughing. There he met
the old goose who, never having seen him laugh before, asked
him the reason for his happiness. After he had told what had
happened the two of them sat down and had supper. While they
were eating their pudding Peter, who was still in a good temper,
said:

'Mrs Goose, next time I want to be something really agree-
able. I'm tired of being, among other things, either a bird or a
fish or an animal. Tell me, my friend, what do you suggest?'

'Upon my word,' the goose answered, 'truthfully I can think
of nothing at the moment. You must realise that there are very
few more eggs, and as you know now the fewer they get the
slower, funnily enough, their magic works.'

'Yes, you don't need to tell me that. But somehow or other I
have the feeling that I would like to be a butterfly. It can't be
very tiring flitting from one flower to another, from a rose, say,
to a lily. What do you think of my idea of being a beautiful
butterfly? I would stay in my own garden, and I think I would
be a decoration to it.'

Mrs Goose, to tell you the truth, was beginning to become
just a little frightened of giving Peter any advice. At last she
said: 'Peter, you must do what you please. From now on I don't
want to be mixed up in anything you wish to be.'

But when Peter had got an idea into his head he could be very
stubborn. So he took the second to last egg, did not hesitate to
wish to be a butterfly and broke the shell. He found himself
lying on a rickety stool. He was a chrysalis and could not move.
After a while a butterfly's head peeped forth and he could see
the old goose facing him.

'What's the matter?' she asked.

'I don't feel very comfortable,' Peter was able to whisper.

'My chest and back are cramped and hurting me. Have I a hump-back? Oh, my arms and legs! Oh, my . . . .'

Peter stopped not knowing what he was going to say next, for the change was now complete and he had become a very lovely blue, yellow and black butterfly. As the window was open he flew out, fluttering in the sunshine and passing the pigsty to find himself in the garden. The goose was waiting there, and flitting from flower to flower the butterfly soon passed close to her.

'What a wonderful life,' Peter said, 'floating about like this, drinking the dew, living on honey and the scent of flowers. I am no longer a boy, and I am not even a butterfly. I am a god.'

'But there is one thing you must remember,' the goose answered, 'and that is that your life is short and you may live only for a day. Good luck does not last for ever, but I suppose it is better to be happy for such a short time than be as miserable as you have been for all of one's life.'

'Bless my soul!' Peter exclaimed. 'You have spoiled my dreams by telling me that I will not live for very long, and if I had my hands I would give you a good thump.'

'Peter, my friend, already your wings are growing weaker and there is not a minute to lose. Wish quickly to become yourself again.'

What had happened was that the goose's words had scared him very badly and he was fluttering towards the grass.

'I want to be myself again! I want to be myself again!' he cried out in panic.

But, as I have told you, the changes were getting slower and slower and a long time had to pass before Peter was to be himself again. Indeed the sun had set before he was able to go back with the goose to the farmhouse. He was aching all over, and when he lay down on his bed he went straight to sleep.

Next morning when he got up he remembered there was only one egg left and that he had to be very careful how he used his last wish. So he went to sit on a bench at the farmhouse door and to ponder on things. He did not notice that the goose had followed him, so he gave a start when he heard her say: 'What are you thinking about, Peter?'

'I was wondering how I should use my last wish.'

'Oh, don't worry too much about that Peter. When you break your last egg you will not even know what you will change into. Don't worry, and please don't ask me for advice for if you did that I would be afraid that something unlucky might happen.'

'But,' Peter asked, 'if I am unhappy about what I am changed into can I change back to myself again?'

'Of course. You know you have always been able to do that.'

'Very well then, and whatever happens don't laugh at me. Up till now I have made such bad choices that it can only be better for me to make another. But if I don't break this last egg I will always be saying to myself that I may have missed some good fortune. All the same, I'm a little scared. However, the egg is in my hand in my pocket and, here goes, I am going to throw it against the wall.'

When the egg smashed Peter felt prickly all over as if thousands of quills were growing through his skin. He slid from the bench where he had been sitting and landed with a pair of large flat feet attached to very short legs. His eyes squinted beside a large yellow beak. Very upset he called out to his friend:

'Good heavens! What sort of a creature have I become!'

'A goose! A goose!' she called out. And as she said this she gave a cackle of laughter.

Peter was furious with anger. 'What's all this about? You are making a fool of me.'

'That's very true,' the goose replied when she had got her breath back. 'You are not only a goose but the silliest goose I have ever seen. You shuffle about clumsily, you have a shrill voice, and you are cross-eyed with fear. Forgive me for laughing at you, Peter, but if you could see yourself you would laugh too.'

As you can imagine, Peter was very upset. He went on shuffling around the farmyard. He wanted very much to be himself again. He wished and he wished in his goose brain, and ever so slowly he changed back. He had learned a nasty lesson and he didn't sleep all that night.

Next morning he put his sickle over his shoulder and was starting off to work in the fields that his parents had left to him.

'Good morning Peter,' said the old goose who was paddling about at the door, 'where are you off to?'

'Can't you see?' Peter answered gruffly. 'I am going out to work.'

'Good gracious me,' Mrs Goose said in a mocking voice, 'wonders will never cease.'

Peter held his head high.

'You silly goose, go back to your friends in the farmyard. I know now how silly I have been in not looking after my farm, and wasting my time always wanting to be different from how I was born. And above all by asking for advice from an old goose who finished up by making me the image of herself. Listen to me, my friend, nothing now will ever make me change my mind – I don't want to dream any more of changing into impossible things. I am going to follow my father and my mother's good example, and I can tell you that I have no other wish.'

And having made that little speech Peter tramped to his fields where he worked very hard, as any young farmer should. From then on he never listened to foolish advice, and never broke another egg unless he was going to eat it for breakfast.

THE KING OF THE MOLES AND
HIS DAUGHTER

At the far end of a small village in Hungary, so small that it is
not shown on any map, there was a thatched cottage where a
poor widow and her son lived. The widow's name was
Madeleine, and her son's was Joseph. A little orchard and
garden, beyond which was a field, were all they owned.

They both worked hard and were able to make a living from
the sale of the fruit and the corn. It is true that life for them was
hard but they were perfectly happy.

From his childhood Joseph had always been a good son. He
loved his mother dearly and looked after her, knowing that he
had never been any worry to her. At the time I am telling you
about he had just had his twentieth birthday. He was a
good-looking young man not quite five feet four inches tall, with
fair curly hair and blue eyes, good white teeth, and a tanned
face. All his life he had been happy and cheerful.

The people in the village did not know anyone who worked
harder than Joseph. If he was not busy in the field he would be
digging in the garden, or looking after the rose-bushes, or
pruning the fruit-trees. He seemed to have time for everything,
and among the pear, apple and peach trees he even found time
to grow flowers.

Often his mother would have liked to help him, if only to
weed the paths or the flower-beds, but with a laugh Joseph
always refused to allow her, saying:

'Mother, you have always been good to me, and I am now
twenty years old. Please sit and rest, but watch me if you like.'

And so Madeleine would sit near him as he worked singing some song or other in praise of Hungary and Marie-Thérèse.

Then, one day, instead of leaving for his work in the morning and returning for his meal of black bread in the evening singing one of his songs, something had happened. From then on he would go into the garden all by himself, finding it very difficult to go back to the cottage. In the evenings he would sit without stirring in a shelter built near the cottage wall and over which he had grown a vine to give his mother protection from the sun.

Joseph seemed to have lost all his old desire to work. Madeleine soon became worried, for she could see her son changing before her eyes and she wondered whether he was ill. But after a time she thought he might have some secret sorrow. She began to follow him into the orchard and one day, hidden behind a fruit-tree, she saw him gazing as if in a dream at a patch of earth as if he was expecting something to come out. She went up to him and, with tears in her eyes, said:

'Joseph, for heaven's sake, if you are feeling ill please tell your mother.'

But he shook his head and forcing a smile replied: 'No, mother, I am perfectly well.' However, as he said this he gave a little sigh.

The sigh encouraged Madeleine to say to him:

'If you are not ill then there must be something else. Tell me about it, for I want to see you happy again, as happy as you always used to be.'

'Mother,' Joseph answered, 'my happiness has gone for ever, and great though your love is for me it can never replace what I have lost.'

Madeleine started to shed bitter tears, for she loved her son more than anything else in the world and would have given him everything that he wished. She was inconsolable, and pleaded with him, and in the end Joseph, very touched, took her in his arms and let fall the words which came from his heart: 'Mother, I am deeply in love.'

When she heard this Madeleine wiped away her tears. She saw Joseph through a mother's eyes, and yet try as she would she could not imagine anyone in the village whom he would wish to marry.

'If that is all that is wrong and has distressed you so much tell me who is the lucky girl, and I will go and call on her parents. Is it Bertha the schoolmaster's daughter, or Marguerite whose father is the Judge?'

'No,' Joseph replied. 'It is neither. If it were only Marguerite or Bertha I wouldn't be so troubled.'

'Oh dear,' said poor Madeleine, 'have you fallen in love with someone much grander than either of those two?'

'Alas, yes.'

'Some nobleman's daughter?'

'If she were only that.'

'A countess?'

'Much higher.'

'A duchess?'

'Much, much higher.'

'Then she must be a princess.'

'Mother,' Joseph nearly shouted, 'mother, I am in love with the daughter of the King of the Moles.'

Madeleine uttered a cry. Then, when she was more composed she said: 'My poor boy, you must be mad.'

'No, mother, unfortunately I am not mad. If I were I would be happy.'

'Joseph, I think we should go to town and see a doctor.'

'Oh, mother, it's not a matter for a doctor. I tell you that I am neither mad nor sick, and to prove it I will tell you how it all happened.'

Madeleine gave a little shake of her head, for she was not reassured by what she had heard her son just say. She feared only the worst. Joseph felt that he knew what was passing through his mother's mind and he was very sorry for her.

'Listen, mother,' he said, 'and I will tell you everything.'

He sat down beside her and took her hands in his.

'Two months ago,' he began, 'one morning when I went to prune the fruit-trees I could not help noticing that the ground among them was covered with molehills. You know how much I dislike these animals which are the despair of all gardeners. That same day I set some traps. But for five or six days I caught nothing. Then, again in the morning, one day I saw a mole sitting on its hill.'

'"Ah!" I cried, grabbing my spade, "you will suffer for them all!"'

'And I lifted my spade to kill it. But you can imagine my astonishment mother when I heard the mole say to me:

'"Don't kill me Joseph. I haven't meant any harm. I am very young, but when I came up just now for a breath of fresh air I understood at once that we have all done wrong. If you spare my life I can promise you that from now on no mole will ever disturb the earth again, neither in your orchard nor your garden."

'The little creature had spoken in so gentle and supplicating a voice and my heart was so touched that I let my spade fall and replied:

'"Of course I will not hurt you."

'"Oh thank you so much," she said, "and if you wish to see me again come here tomorrow evening when the full moon rises and I will tell you something in secret."'

'When she had finished speaking she disappeared into the earth. I very much wished to see her again so that I could hear what she had to tell me, but I was rather frightened for never before had I heard of a mole that talked. At first I longed to tell you what had happened, but I decided to wait until she had spoken to me again, for after all there seemed to be no hurry.

'Next evening I went into the orchard to wait for the moon to rise, and stood at the exact spot where the mole had disappeared into the earth. The moon rose but she did not appear. I thought then that she had been making fun of me, and I was

almost ready to go back to our cottage feeling very sad that our
second meeting had not taken place.

'Then, looking behind me, I saw rise from a big rose-bush the
most beautiful young girl. Her hair was black and hung below
her shoulders, and she wore a crown made of gold-leaf. Her
eyes were dark, too, and as soft as velvet. She had long
eyelashes and arched black eyebrows. She was wearing a robe
which reached her feet and was held at her waist by a golden
girdle. The sleeves of her robe were open to show her pure
white arms. The moon was high in the sky and could let me see
how very beautiful she was.

' "Who are you?" I asked, "and how did you get here?" '

' "I have just come out of the earth," she answered with a
smile".'

' "You have come out of the earth?" '

' "Yes, I am the mole whose life you spared yesterday, and I
have come to thank you for doing that!" '

'I stood there unable to move and thought that I was
dreaming.'

' "I said yesterday that I had a secret to tell you",' she went
on and, all ears, I listened to what she had to tell me.

' "I am the only child of the King of the Moles and will inherit
all his fortune," she said. "I am really and truly a human being
just like you, but a wicked magician changed us into moles
and now we live just like ordinary moles. Only, each time the
moon is full I am allowed to become once more as I used to be
from the hour it rises until it goes down again. But my father
was not granted the same favour and will always stay as
he is." '

'I felt my heart leap to this lovely young girl and that my life
was in her hands.

' "Oh," I said to her, "now that I know that I saved your life
as a mole, do, please, whenever the moon is full, spend as much
time with me as you are now." '

' "Don't ask me that," she replied, "for that might bring you bad luck. It is always dangerous for humans to associate with such poor creatures as ourselves. Believe me, it is for your own good that I refuse to meet you again. Goodbye. Think of me no more.'''

'Then she stepped onto a molehill and started slowly to disappear into the ground. When I saw her leaving me like this I stretched out my arms to try and stop her, but by this time she had vanished. Since that day, or rather since that night, mother, I have never seen her again. But I am always in the orchard; that is why I do not stay inside the cottage at night. I am always hoping that I will see that marvellous vision of beauty again, and that is why I am so sad for I am madly in love with her.

'I think you will understand now after what I have told you that is why I have been so quiet and have spoken to you so little.'

'Joseph! Joseph!' his mother cried. 'What *are* you talking about! How can you fall in love with a mole even if she is the daughter of a king? And, what is worse, wish to marry a being who can be human for only one night a month and for the rest of the month a mole? How do you know that she is not a sorceress who has been sent to tempt you?'

'All I can say, mother, is that I pray that I shall see her again.'

'I think you have seen all this in your dreams.'

'No, mother, I have really and truly seen the daughter of the King of the Moles changed into a human being like you and me, and whom I love most dearly.'

'Try to forget it all, Joseph my dear son. There are plenty of nice girls in the village, and even though we haven't much money people respect us. Go on working in the orchard and soon you will forget all about this, and all will be well.'

But Joseph lowered his head when he heard what his mother had just said and smiled sorrowfully. He knew that her advice was good and that he should do as she said, but he had neither the power nor the wish to forget the lovely young girl with the golden girdle and the crown.

The second full moon since Joseph had first met the daughter of the King of the Moles was now due, and as it drew nearer the more he longed to see the girl he loved so much. He was happier now and worked hard in the garden and orchard. But Madeleine, knowing what had happened before, was very nervous.

The night arrived. Madeleine wanted Joseph to stay indoors, but he replied that for all the money in the world nothing would stop him from going to the orchard.

'Very well,' his mother said, 'I am going with you.'

'Then please keep well away from me if you are determined to come.'

Evening fell. Madeleine sat down in the shelter near the cottage wall and Joseph stood near the trunk of an apple-tree. All Madeleine could do was to weep silently, not letting her son out of sight. Joseph had his eyes fixed on the ground.

The moon suddenly appeared over some far distant mountain, and at once four feet away from where Joseph was standing a molehill started to form, growing bigger and bigger until it was almost all of six or eight feet high. Then it split down the middle, and instead of a lovely girl appearing there came out an enormous mole which seemed in the moonlight to be as big as an ox. It marched towards Joseph.

Madeleine gave a frightened cry and ran towards Joseph to pull him away, but he didn't move a muscle and stayed rooted to the ground.

'Mother, mother,' he said, 'it is the King of the Moles. Don't you recognise him by the crown he is wearing?'

And, as a matter of fact, the mole was wearing a golden crown which glittered in the moonlight.

By now the mole was very close to them both. He stood on his hind legs, and then finally sat down with a very important air. He stretched out to Joseph a large front paw which seemed to have claws on it, and said to him in a very gruff voice:

'Come with me. You will be my son-in-law. Come. My daughter awaits you.'

He put his paw on one of Joseph's shoulders, intending to encourage him to hurry. But Madeleine threw her arms around her son and called out:

'Oh Joseph! Think of your mother, and do not go with this monster!'

Joseph, indeed, was more than a little scared by the size of the mole and very much wished to take her hand and run away with his mother. But just as he turned away from the King of the Moles there came out from the molehill the same girl with the flowing black hair. In her sweet voice she said only one word: 'Joseph.'

Joseph stood still, fascinated. He could not resist that voice and this, together with the smile she gave him, would have broken any resistance. He stayed motionless. But this would not do, for the daughter of the King of the Moles was quite determined that he should follow her. So, in a voice even sweeter and gentler than when she had first uttered his name, she said: 'Come with me.'

Hearing her speak again Joseph tore himself away from his mother and rushed into the princess's arms. Almost at once they both disappeared. In his turn the King of the Moles slowly sank into the ground stopping as he did so the unhappy Madeleine from following her son as she wished to.

The moon had now gone down, and Madeleine fell in a faint on the grass.

When she became conscious again it was dawn and people in the village were stirring. She shed many tears, and her sobbing was so loud that a great many of the villagers came running to ask her what was the matter. She told them all that had happened and what she had seen with her very eyes. They were all terror-stricken, although at first they could not believe her.

But her story rang so true, and her tears were so real, that they were at last convinced. Further, when they saw poor Madeleine scraping the ground with her hands, they went for picks and spades to dig a hole, for of course the molehill had quite disappeared. All was in vain, and Madeleine could not be consoled.

'Oh, good heavens!' she cried. 'If only my son were dead instead of going down into the earth with those dreadful monsters and has now, perhaps, been changed into a mole like themselves.'

Her grief was great, and the good people of the village tried to comfort her by telling her that they would keep on digging until they found her son. Indeed, they dug so deep that they reached an underground stream which stopped them digging any further. They had found nothing – neither Joseph, nor the King of the Moles, nor his daughter.

One year followed another and Madeleine did not stop lamenting the loss of her much-loved son. The orchard, the garden and the field were never looked after as they had been, and weeds grew everywhere. Madeleine herself would have died of hunger if the good people of the village had not brought her food.

One evening when she was sitting outside her cottage wrapped in her own sad thoughts she was quite surprised when she became aware that darkness had fallen. As it happened that was the night of the full moon. It was just rising, and suddenly not far from where she sat a molehill formed and out of it stepped the princess.

As soon as she saw her Madeleine cried: 'Ah, it is you, you wretched woman! Have you come to bring back my son?'

'You will see him again,' the princess answered in her gentle voice, 'but to do so you must follow me into our kingdom.'

'And if I do *will* you promise to let me see him?' Madeleine asked sternly.

'I promise. Follow me.'

'I will. This very instant,' Madeleine cried.

'Then hurry,' the princess said.

Together they went to the top of the molehill and, at once, they disappeared underground. For a minute or two Madeleine lost all sense of being alive, but when she had recovered her wits she found herself in a sort of palace built out of clods of earth piled high on each other, and which teemed with moles of all sizes. She was very much afraid, but the thought of seeing Joseph again soon gave her courage.

'Joseph!' she called out. 'Where are you? I want to see you.'

It was then that the King of the Moles appeared. He touched a kind of curtain which parted, and Joseph fell into his mother's arms. Only these words were spoken:

'My son!'

'Mother!'

Madeleine was the first to recover her speech and she said: 'At last I have seen you again and nothing now will ever part us. Come with me back to our cottage and garden.'

But Joseph only shook his head.

'What!' his mother said in a startled voice. 'Can't you answer me?'

After a few moments Joseph replied. 'Mother,' he said sorrowfully, 'I cannot go with you even if I wished to.'

'How! You are not able? And what is stopping you then? Is it the king? If that is so I will beg him to allow you to come back with me.'

Indeed, Madeleine went on her knees before the King of the Moles and with hands joined together:

'Your majesty,' she entreated, 'please give me back my son. You are a father and will know how heart-breaking it is to be separated from a child. If you don't grant my prayer then I will know that besides being blind moles have no hearts.'

'Truly,' the King of the Moles replied, 'I feel very sorry for you, but you are wrong, for moles have feelings like human beings. But your son cannot leave here because tomorrow he is marrying my daughter.'

'Heaven have mercy on me,' Madeleine sobbed. 'I never imagined that a son of mine I have brought up so carefully would marry a mole princess. No, no, he must never do that. You *must* give him back to me and I will take him home. Otherwise I will die.'

'Listen,' said the king, 'if you don't wish him to be parted from you then you must live here with us all.'

'I would be very frightened to live here, but I suppose that if I am beside Joseph I would get used to it and be happy.'

'Yes, stay here mother,' Joseph interrupted, 'because if you do, nothing would make me happier.'

'But there is one condition I must impose,' the King of the Moles continued.

'And what is that?' Madeleine asked.

'We moles,' the king went on, 'are, as you have just said, blind.'

'Well?' And Madeleine was becoming more frightened than ever.

'You must become blind like the rest of us.'

'That's dreadful, for if I were to become blind I would not be able to see my son.'

'That is true,' the king answered, 'but you would be near him, he loves you, and you would be able to touch him and hear his voice.'

'But I want to go on seeing him,' Madeleine pleaded. 'For years I have dreamed of seeing him again. I will only look at *him* and not at anyone else.'

'No,' the king replied, 'you have no other choice. Otherwise you will go back to earth and never see or hear your son again.'

'Never! Never!' Madeleine cried out. 'I cannot, and will not, ever leave my son. Make me blind like the rest of you and let me stay near him. I only ask that when you do this to me I may hold him by the hand so that he does not leave me a second time.'

'Certainly,' said the King of the Moles, 'your request is granted.'

Joseph knelt before his mother and took her hands which he pressed against his lips. Tears ran from his eyes. When Madeleine saw them she quickly dried them and said: 'Don't cry, Joseph, for I am very happy.'

And to make him believe that she was, indeed, happy she tried hard and succeeded in smiling.

Meanwhile, two moles were blowing on a fire to make the flames shoot higher as another pair heated two needles. Madeleine half-turned to watch them and shivered with fright. Then she gazed at her son with great love as if she wished to engrave the memory of his face on her heart.

'If you are ready,' she said to the moles, 'I am.'

It was then that the king asked: 'Madam, do you wish to change your mind? You are quite free to do so, for it is not too late.'

'Do what you wish. Even if I cannot see him I will at least be beside my son.' And she looked again at Joseph with extraordinary tenderness, holding him in her arms.

The two moles walked towards her and, then, standing on their hind legs brought the needles close to Madeleine's eyes.

But at the moment when the needles touched her eyelids there was a great clap of thunder which made the earth shake, and the palace of the moles fell in ruins. Madeleine was bewildered, for she could not understand what had happened. She found herself lying in her son's arms and opened her eyes in terror fearful that she might not be able to see. But she could see clearly, and what she saw was a tall handsome man in a purple robe with a golden crown on his head.

Close beside him was the beautiful princess looking just as she had done when she appeared three times before on earth. Many lords and ladies, all richly dressed, were near the radiant pair.

The earthen palace had gone and in its place was a splendid one all made of marble, and which was no longer under the ground but stood gleaming in the sunshine. All was happiness and gaiety.

I am sure you will ask as Madeleine did. 'What has happened?', as she stared about her thinking she was dreaming.

Then the man in the purple robe spoke.

'I was the King of the Moles', he said. 'A wicked magician in a fit of spite turned me and my court and my subjects into moles. We were all forced to live deep underground until some human, to prove her great love for her son, would agree to be made blind, like us, and to live among us. For two thousand years we have prayed for deliverance. We had lured some humans into our earthen palace, but none of them had your devotion and courage. You have freed us and you will be rewarded.

'Your son loves my daughter, and I give her to him as his bride. One day he will succeed me as king. The wicked magician from now onwards can do us no harm, for it is he who has taken my place. The magician is now living beneath the ground with all his cruel family. You, madam, will always stay in our palace with us, and we will forever be grateful to you.'

But Madeleine shook her head.

'Your majesty,' she replied, 'I am not used to living in all this luxury and splendour. Thank you very much for your kind words and for your invitation, but if you wish to make me happy all I ask of you is to allow me to live very simply near my son in a small thatched cottage with a garden. Then I will be rewarded, for I will be able to see him every day and rejoice in his happiness. That would be my greatest reward. As for what I have done it was for the love of my son, and if you have waited so very long to be freed it is because you never thought of asking for a mother's help.'

Joseph married his beautiful princess. They were very happy, and when Joseph came to the throne he devoted his whole life to the well-being of his subjects.

Madeleine lived on for another twenty-five years in the cottage that the former King of the Moles had had built for her. Her greatest pleasure was to sit in her garden watching her grandchildren growing up.

THE MAGIC WHISTLE

There once lived a rich and powerful king who had a daughter who was quite remarkable for her marvellous beauty. When she reached the age at which she could marry the king announced by the blowing of trumpets, as well as by posters placed on the walls of his capital, that those who wanted her hand should gather in a large field. The princess would then throw high into the air a golden apple, and whoever succeeded in catching it would then have to solve three problems. As the king had no son the one who was successful could then marry the princess and, in the fullness of time, inherit the kingdom.

On the chosen day the competitors gathered. The princess threw the apple, but not one of the first three who caught it was able to solve the easiest problem, and not one of them even tried those that followed. Finally, when the golden apple was thrown for the fourth time it was caught by a young shepherd who was certainly the most handsome of the competitors but who was, unluckily, the poorest of them all.

The first problem, then, that he was asked to solve, and it certainly was made as difficult for him as any you will find in your arithmetic books, was this:

The king had kept locked up in a stable a hundred hares, and if he succeeded in taking them out to feed next morning into the field where the competition had been held, and then lead them all back to the stable in the evening, he would have solved the first problem.

When the young shepherd was told this he asked to be given a day to think things over, and he would then reply 'yes' or 'no'.

This request seemed so fair to the king that permission was granted.

The shepherd at once set out to a neighbouring forest, there to think of some way of carrying out the task he had been given. He was slowly walking along a narrow path running beside a stream, with his head bent down in deepest thought, when he met a little old woman with white hair and very bright eyes who asked him why he was so sad.

Shaking his head the shepherd answered: 'Alas, no one can help me. And yet I very much wish to marry the king's daughter.'

'Don't give away to despair so quickly,' the old woman replied. 'Tell me what your troubles are and, you never know, I may be able to help you.'

The shepherd's heart was so heavy that he was only too willing to tell her everything.

'Is that all you have to worry about?' the old woman asked. 'If that is so you have no need to despair.'

And she took from a pocket in her dress an ivory whistle and handed it to him.

The whistle was just like any other whistle, and thinking that it might have to be blown in some special way he turned to ask the old woman, but she had already disappeared. However, full of confidence in what he had come to think of as some good fairy, he went along next day to the palace and said to the king:

'Sir, I accept, and have come for the hares so that I may take them to the field.'

Hearing this the king stood up and said to one of his ministers: 'Have the hares turned out of the stable.'

The shepherd stood at the stable door to count them, but the first had already vanished into the distance by the time the last one was out. Indeed, when he reached the field there was not a single hare in sight. He sat down thoughtfully, not daring to believe in the magic qualities of his whistle. But as there was only one resort left to him he put the whistle to his lips and blew as hard as he could. The whistle gave forth a shrill and very long note.

At once, to his great astonishment, there came running to him from right and left, from in front of him and from behind him, the hundred hares which all set to work to browse quietly around him.

The king was told what had happened, of how the young shepherd had solved the problem of the hundred hares, and he talked the matter over with his daughter. Both were very cross, for if the young man succeeded in solving the remaining two problems as promptly as he had solved the first then the princess would become the wife of a poor peasant, and nothing could be more humiliating to royal pride than that.

'It is best,' said the princess to her father, 'that you deal with the matter as you see fit, and I will think things over.'

The princess went to her room and disguised herself in such a way that no one could know who she was. Then she had a horse saddled for her, mounted it, and rode to the shepherd.

The hares were still frisking happily about him.

'Will you sell me one of your hares?' she asked him.

'I wouldn't sell one of my hares for all the money in the world,' he answered, 'but you may win one.'

'And what would I have to do?'

'You must get off your horse and sit beside me on the grass for a quarter of an hour.'

The princess didn't like the idea very much, but as there was no other way of getting the hare she got off her horse and sat down beside the shepherd. During the next fifteen minutes the young man said any number of tender things to her. When the time came she rose and claimed her hare, and faithful to his promise she was given one.

Joyfully the princess shut it in a basket attached to her saddle-bow and started riding back to the palace. But she had hardly ridden a mile when the shepherd put his whistle to his lips and blew. Hearing the command the hare forced open the lid of the basket, sprang to the ground, and ran back as fast as its legs could carry it.

A few minutes later the shepherd saw a peasant coming towards him riding a donkey. It was the king, also disguised, who had left the palace with the same idea as his daughter. A large sack was hanging from the donkey's saddle.

'Will you sell me one of your hares?' he asked the shepherd.

'My hares are not for sale,' was the reply, 'but you may win one.'

'And what have I to do?'

'You must stop your donkey's tail from twitching and then kiss it three times,' the shepherd said at last.

This very odd condition did not appeal to the king at all. He tried as hard as he could to avoid agreeing, even going so far as to offer fifty thousand francs for one of the hares, but the shepherd would not change his terms.

At last the king, who was quite determined to get a hare, agreed to do what he was asked, humiliating as it was for one who wore a crown. Three times he kissed the donkey's tail, and the donkey was greatly surprised at the honour done to him. Faithful to his word the shepherd gave the king a hare.

The king stuffed the hare into the sack and rode off as fast as his donkey could carry him. But he, also, had hardly gone a mile when a whistle sounded and, hearing it, the hare scratched so hard at the sack that he made a hole in it through which he jumped and fled.

'Well?' the princess asked, when she saw that the king had returned to the palace.

'I hardly know what to say, my daughter,' the king replied. 'This fellow is so obstinate that he refused to sell me a hare at any price. But don't worry, he will not so easily solve the other two problems as he did the first.'

It goes without saying that the king did not tell his daughter of the condition by which he got possession of one of the hares for such a brief time, and neither did the princess mention anything about the terms of her own unsuccess. All she said was that she could not induce the shepherd to part with one of the hares for either gold or silver.

That evening the shepherd returned with the hares. He counted them in the king's presence and there was neither one more nor one less than the original hundred, and they were put back in the royal stable.

Then the king said: 'The first problem has been solved, and now there is the second. Listen carefully, young man.'

The shepherd listened with the greatest attention.

'Over there, in my granary,' the king continued, 'there are a hundred bushels of peas and the same number of lentils. They are all mixed together. If you can succeed tonight, in darkness, in dividing them into separate heaps then you have solved the second problem.'

'I shall do my best,' the shepherd replied.

And the king had the young man taken to the granary. He was locked in, and the key was given back to the king.

It was already night, and as for such a task there was no time to be lost the shepherd took his whistle and blew it. At once five thousand ants appeared. They all set to work separating the lentils from the peas, and never stopped until they were divided into two heaps.

On the following morning the king went to the granary and to his great amazement saw that everything had been done as he had commanded. He tried to find excuses, but hard as he tried there was nothing he could find wrong. All that he could do now was to rely on the third problem which, after the shepherd's two successes, did not give him very much hope.

However, as this third problem was the most difficult of them all the king did not despair altogether.

'What now remains for you to do,' he said, 'is to go when twilight falls into the palace bread-pantry, and during the night eat the whole week's supply of bread stored there. If tomorrow morning not a single crumb remains I will be happy to let you marry my daughter.'

So when evening came the shepherd was led to the bread-pantry which was, indeed, so stacked with bread that there was only a very small space near the door which was empty.

But at midnight when all was quiet in the palace the shepherd once again took his whistle and blew it. It was only a matter of moments before ten thousand mice set to work nibbling at the bread so fast that by the time morning arrived not a single crumb was left. It was then that the young man hammered on the door with all his strength, and called out: 'Hurry up and open the door, please! I'm hungry!'

And so, just as the others had been, the third problem was victoriously solved. The king, nevertheless, tried hard to get out of his bargain. He had brought to him a sack that was big enough to hold six bushels of corn. Then he summoned a great many of his palace staff and said to the shepherd in front of them:

'Tell me in front of all these people as many falsehoods as will fill this sack. When it is quite full then you can marry my daughter.'

The shepherd then repeated all the untruths he could think of, but half the day had gone with the sack still far from being full, and he was at his wit's end to think of more.

After thinking very hard for some time he said: 'Well, while I was guarding the hares the princess came along disguised as a peasant and, to get one of them, she allowed me to kiss her.'

The princess, who was also present and had not the slightest suspicion of what the shepherd would say, blushed as red as a cherry. The king began to believe that there might just possibly be some truth in what the young man had said, but hastily interrupted:

'Although you have dropped a very big falsehood into the sack it is not yet full. Go on.'

The shepherd bowed and continued: 'A few minutes after the

princess had left me I saw your majesty, disguised as a peasant too, and riding a donkey. Your majesty came to buy one of your own hares. Now, seeing that you were very eager to do so can you imagine what I asked you to do . . . ?'

'Enough! Enough!' shouted the king. 'The sack is full!'

A week later the young shepherd married the princess.

THE END